MAGIC
DELIVERY

Other books by Clete Barrett Smith

The Intergalactic Bed & Breakfast Series

Aliens on Vacation
Alien on a Rampage
Aliens in Disguise

MAGIC
DELIVERY

By
CLETE BARRETT SMITH

With illustrations by
MICHAŁ DZIEKAN

DISNEp • HYPERION BOOKS
LOS ANGELES   NEW YORK

First Edition

1 3 5 7 9 10 8 6 4 2

G475-5664-5-14135

Printed in the United States of America

Library of Congress Cataloging-in-Publication Data
Smith, Clete Barrett.
    Magic delivery / by Clete Barrett Smith ; with
illustrations by Michal Dziekan.—First edition.
        pages cm
    Summary: "When two boys stumble upon a seemingly abandoned
truckload of costumes, they think they have hit the jackpot. There's just
one small catch: The costumes are bewitched"—Provided by publisher.
    ISBN 978-1-4231-6597-2
    [1. Costume—Fiction. 2. Magic—Fiction. 3. Monsters—
Fiction.] I. Dziekan, Michal, illustrator. II. Title.
    PZ7.S644633Mag 2014
    [Fic]—dc23   2013022020

Reinforced binding

Visit www.DisneyBooks.com

This one is for my Cameo

PART I

THE MAGIC HALLOWEEN COSTUMES

NICK STRINGER CONCENTRATED ON HIS TEST, NOT because he cared about Shakespeare (he didn't) and not because he wanted to get all the answers right (that was too easy). But because missing a few—strategically—paid the bills.

It had all started when Nick learned that Tania Hillington's parents promised her a reward of sixty dollars for earning the highest grade in any class on any test. (*Sixty dollars!*) So he offered to botch a few of his test answers to help her out. In exchange for a fifty-fifty split of the reward, of course.

Tania had declined. At first.

Things changed after Nick aced five consecutive tests. Tania came crawling back to accept the deal. But by that point the terms had changed. Their little arrangement now operated on a seventy-thirty split in Nick's favor.

Then there was Tommy, the dim-witted linebacker. He needed a C-minus just to keep his head above the waterline of Bayside Middle School's athletic policy. He gave Nick a few bucks to skip all extra-credit questions so as not to blow the grading curve.

And Nick had other customers today. Three more jocks, plus this guy who was one academic pink slip away from a trip to Saturday school, and, finally, a girl who was convinced that Harvard would scour her middle school transcripts for any signs of a dreaded A-minus. They all had the same class in the afternoon and would buy original outlines for the essay question from Nick at lunch.

All told, he figured to make a cool hundred on this test. Not bad.

Nick finished early and checked over his "work," erasing two more correct answers and finding a new way to misspell *embarrass*. Burger, meanwhile, was staring holes into his own test. Beads of sweat seeped through that shaggy mop of blond hair to drip down his forehead as he made little grunting noises in concentration. School was not designed for people like Burger.

Nick nudged his answer sheet to the edge of the desk. Only Burger got a freebie. He looked up at Nick with puppylike gratitude, then rushed to copy as many answers as he could before Mr. Ritzeller called time.

Bored, Nick let his eyes wander across the test

questions again. Just to pass the time, he reread the one about the "stratified society." Apparently back in Shakespeare's day only rich people were allowed—by law—to wear clothes of certain colors and materials. Like you could be thrown in jail for wearing purple or silk or something. Mr. Ritzeller said back then you could walk down the street and tell, simply by looking, which social class anyone belonged to.

As Nick scanned the classroom, he knew that nothing had changed. While his classmates' fashion choices weren't mandated by law, you could still tell at a glance where each kid came from. Mall-bought, brand-name clothes on one side, thrift-store denim and flannel on the other.

Bayside Middle School drew students from two areas: Bayside Gardens, a gated community on the south side with a private golf course and houses right on the water, and Smoke Valley, where people worked either at the mill or at the Hungry Lumberjack, the restaurant across the street from the mill.

Little Miss Sixty-Per-Test Tania lived in a house that had wraparound decks on all four stories to take advantage of the spectacular view of the San Juan Islands. Nick's bedroom window had a view of the bushes where his dog went to the bathroom.

When the bell finally rang, Burger jumped out of his seat as if it were electrified and rumbled down the aisle, his oversize denim-and-flannel-clad frame knocking into chairs and backpacks and anyone who was smaller than he was (which is to say everyone, including Mr. Ritzeller). Close spaces were not designed for people like Burger.

The two boys were headed to the cafeteria when Hayley Millard herself approached in a tight cashmere sweater and designer jeans. She glanced around warily, as if afraid that everyone always noticed what the richest of the richies was doing at every moment, but people just sort of bustled by. Burger's mouth hung open as he stared. He was noticing her enough for the entire school.

"Hey, it's Nick, right?" Hayley said without exactly making eye contact.

Yes, Hayley, we've been in most of the same classes since kindergarten.

"Some friends told me I should, you know, get in touch with you or whatever." She cleared her throat, glanced at the ground. "They said you're the kind of person who might be able to, like, help me."

Nick raised his eyebrows a bit but just stood there, waiting. First rule in business negotiations: He Who Speaks First Loses. You had to let the other person keep talking until they had told you what they wanted, putting you in a position of power.

"I sort of have a problem."

More waiting from Nick. (More staring from Burger.)

"Mr. Glover is doing one of his extended labs this afternoon. Worth a ton of points." Hayley twirled a thick lock of auburn hair between her fingers.

Nick made a *keep-going* gesture.

"I'm totally unprepared. And I'm going to fail Bio if I bomb that lab. Stupid fruit flies." She chewed on her lower lip. "And then I'll be grounded for, like, *months*. My mom will make me cancel my Halloween party this weekend, for sure."

Nick nodded. "And...?"

Hayley shot a narrow-eyed glance at Burger, who at least had the decency to wipe the drool from his chin.

"It's okay," Nick said. "He can hear anything you have to say."

She looked back over at Nick and lowered her voice. "Any chance you could get the lab postponed? Just until Monday?"

And there it was.

Nick shrugged. "What's it worth to you?"

It was his favorite question. And he couldn't wait to hear what Hayley came up with. She not only looked rich, she *smelled* like money.

Hayley glanced around the hall again, made sure no one was listening. "I could give you...I don't know, I've never done this before...how about fifty bucks?" When he didn't say anything right away, Hayley rushed to fill the silence with a better offer. "Okay, maybe a hundred? But that's it. That's all I have on me."

A hundred dollars. Even though he had been taking the Southsiders' money for years, Nick was still amazed sometimes by how much cash they had to throw around.

He kept up his poker face, though, as always. Unskilled negotiators hated silence, so Nick used it as a weapon. After a few more uncomfortably quiet moments, Hayley rummaged through her purse. "Okay, there's the cash, plus...let's see...plus a gift card that you can use anywhere at the mall...and, oh yeah, here's a packet of free tickets that are good for any movie playing at that new theater downtown." She held up a handful of random purse fodder and attempted a half smile. "But I guess the lipstick and contact-lens holder won't work too well for a bribe." The smile was kind of nice. A little crooked. Nice to know everything about her wasn't totally perfect.

No time to think about that, though. Nick pretended to be deciding, but he would have done it for just the hundred. Heck, he would have done it for the original offer of fifty. The truth was, he actually wanted to help her out. Had wanted to have a good reason to talk to her ever since that kindergarten class. Maybe it would even lead to her talking to him sometime when she didn't need a favor? A guy could dream.

But now he had to take care of business. Hayley had broken the second rule of negotiations: Never Talk Past the Close. These rich kids were such amateurs.

Nick held out his palm to accept the goods when—

"And invite us to your party," Burger blurted out.

Hayley looked up from her purse. "Excuse me?"

When Burger got embarrassed, the blotches on his

cheeks bypassed pink and even red to become almost purple in contrast with his whitish-blond hair. Social interaction—especially with the opposite sex—was not designed for people like Burger.

"That big Halloween party. This weekend," Burger said. "We wanna come, too."

Hayley crinkled up her nose and shot Nick an annoyed glance. He would never have forced an invitation like that —this was business, not personal—but he had to admit it would be pretty cool to actually attend a party at the Millard estate.

Nick shrugged again. "You can keep the movie tickets."

Hayley checked her surroundings once more. "I don't even know if my mom will let me invite anyone else over. There probably won't be enough room."

Nick stifled a laugh. Everyone in school knew about Hayley's house. So did anyone with a subscription to *Architectural Digest*. The entire student body would probably fit in the east wing alone.

Time for Hayley's last lesson in negotiations: The Takeaway. "Good luck with that lab," he said, dropping his palm and walking away. Burger stayed where he was for a few moments, confused, before he clomped down the hall to join his friend.

"Why did you—"

"Don't look back," Nick whispered.

"What are you doing?" Burger said, too loudly. "That's a lot of cash, dude."

"She's deciding whether she wants to have a party with us there or have no party at all because she's grounded."

"But what if she doesn't—"

"Stop talking."

When they were about to turn the corner, Hayley called out behind them, "Hey—just a minute." She waited for a group of guys from the cross-country team to pass and drift out of earshot, and then she approached. "Fine. You can come to the party."

Something in Nick's stomach did a nervous little happy dance at that news, but he kept his face calm and cool.

She thrust a handful of bills at Nick, then leaned forward to whisper, "Just make sure he wears something with a mask. Hopefully one without a mouth hole so he can't talk." She tossed her auburn hair back over one shoulder with a flip of her head. "Or at least something, you know, low profile. That's all I'm asking."

Nick tried to muster up some righteous indignation on his friend's behalf, but there was really no place for that in a business interaction. "Sure," he whispered back. "Maybe I can find him an Invisible Man costume."

There was that lopsided little half smile again. "If I could buy a costume like that, I wouldn't need your help with the biology lab. I could just sneak out, totally unseen." Then she winked at him. Nick's face got a little warm. He was glad that Hayley didn't seem to know her own power. A wink like that could seriously derail a negotiation. She gave him a little wave and then turned and walked away. "Just make sure I'm not covered in fruit flies sixth period," she said over her shoulder.

Burger watched those jeans until they disappeared around the next corner.

"Dude. You actually talked to Hayley Millard."

"And she talked back. I think that's called a conversation, Burger."

"Did she say something about me when she whispered?"

Nick nodded. "She's excited about you coming to her party."

"Nice!" Burger pumped his fist in triumph.

"She wants you to wear something flashy. Noticeable. Maybe a skintight superhero costume?"

"I still got that Wolverine outfit from fourth grade."

"The bright yellow one?"

"Yep."

"Perfect."

2

NICK COUNTED THE WAD OF BILLS AS HE LED Burger toward the science wing.

"So..." Burger nudged him, eyebrows waggling. "What are you gonna do with all that cash?"

"Same thing I always do with it." Nick didn't tell anyone the truth about his money. Not even Burger.

"The bank? Again?" Burger shook his head, that flyaway mess of blond hair flopping in all directions. "But we could buy so much cool stuff. How much is in that savings account, anyway? Gotta be thousands by now."

Nick tapped his chin and looked up at the ceiling as they walked down the hall, making a show out of thinking it over. "With today's haul, I think there's finally going to be enough for the surgery."

Burger looked at him with an expression of such intense, genuine concern that Nick almost felt guilty. Burger lowered his voice to a husky whisper. "Dude. What do you need surgery for?"

"Not for me. For you." He patted Burger's meaty shoulder. "That brain transplant is going to be a real life-changer."

Burger casually shifted his considerable weight and bodychecked Nick into a row of lockers. "Whoops."

A couple of Bayside Garden girls walked by and didn't even glance at Nick as he went sprawling to the floor. Sometimes Nick thought that getting picked on at school would be better than the Southsiders' total indifference. But unless the rich kids needed something, he and Burger were pretty much invisible.

Still, Nick tried to muster up a little dignity as he collected the scattered books and rubbed at his sore elbow. "See what I mean? That new brain is really going to help your balance problems."

Burger lunged sideways to sideswipe him again, but Nick stopped suddenly and Burger lurched off balance and crashed into the lockers himself. One of the girls glanced over her shoulder and shook her head in disgust before turning back away.

Nick smiled. At least he and Burger had officially existed for a few seconds.

The boys approached the double doors of the science wing. Lindsay McDonald, a long-legged eighth grader, sat in front of the doors on a stool, lunch tray balanced on her lap. She was a Smoke Valley girl, and Nick knew that she guarded the science wing each day as hall monitor in exchange for free school lunch.

"Hey, guys."

"Hi, Lindsay!" Burger said.

Nick just raised his eyebrows and inclined his head toward the closed doors.

"Sorry. Nobody goes in here during lunch." She wiped the corner of her mouth with a napkin. "You know that, Nick."

"But I brought an official hall pass." Nick took a ten-dollar bill from his jeans pocket. "I only need to be in there for a few minutes, so you should just keep the pass."

Lindsay looked at the money, then cracked open the science-wing doors and scanned the hallway before returning her attention to the lunch tray. "This is a high-security area. It's going to take two more hall passes if you want in."

Smoke Valley kids were always better negotiators than the Southsiders. He pulled out another ten along with a five. "That makes two and a half hall passes. We just need five minutes."

"Fine." Lindsay swiped the money from Nick's hand. "But anything past five minutes and I call the vice principal."

"No need for that."

"I could get in trouble, Nick."

He sighed. Man, she was good. Setting up a new deal right after closing the last one. "Look, how about another hall pass for every minute longer than five?"

"Done."

Nick and Burger slipped through the doors into the empty hall. "Have a seat," Nick said, pointing to the bench. "If any teachers show up, you need to create some sort of distraction. Can you still do that thing where you fake an asthma attack?"

Burger wheezed and gripped his chest. Purple blotches spread out across his broad cheeks. He slumped in his chair, eyes bulging and breath rattling in his throat.

"Easy on the death rattle, big fella. We want an extra minute for me to get away, not to have you airlifted to the hospital in an emergency helicopter."

"That'd be so fun, though," Burger said. But he did take his performance down a notch, his breathing now just a little ragged as he groped in his pockets with growing desperation in search for an inhaler that wasn't there.

Nick nodded. "That's perfect. It'll freak out any adult, but not too much. They'll just take you to the nurse's office." He turned toward the door to Mr. Glover's biology lab. There was a number pad next to the handle; the science wing needed high-tech locks to protect all of that expensive equipment.

Nick punched in a five-number code and the handle turned smoothly under his hand. Over half of the teachers used their home addresses for entry codes or passwords. At least Glover had gotten a little creative and used his daughter's birthday. Nick had figured it out on the first day of school, after spending a little time on Facebook. Just in case.

As he stepped into the darkened room, Burger called his name. Nick snapped his head around, scanning the hallway, but it was still empty.

"What is it?" he whispered.

"You need a *face* transplant." Burger grinned.

Nick rolled his eyes. "Might want to work on your timing, Burger."

Easing the door shut behind him, Nick weighed his options. The easiest solution would be to pop the aquarium's lid and offer the fruit flies a taste of glorious freedom. That would certainly postpone the lab.

But it was no good. The entire class would have to be moved to a holding area, like the library, while the custodian cleaned out the swarm of flies. Glover would be furious. He'd get the vice principal to check the security tapes from the hallway, for sure.

Besides, this was a business transaction with Hayley, not a revenge mission against Glover. The situation was a little more delicate, called for something discreet. Nick approached Glover's desk to log on to the computer.

Enter password

Nick typed in *paramecium9*. That one was a little trickier; it had taken him almost a week to figure it out.

It shouldn't have been that difficult, though. Glover

had taken photos of the single-celled critters through a microscope, enlarged the images, and taped them all over his classroom walls the way some guys hang up posters of hot girls. Teachers were so weird.

Nick searched the hard drive and found Glover's file on fruit flies, with documents for the lab setup, assignment work sheets, and the quiz. First he printed the pages out and shoved them in the pocket of his jeans. Some grade-grubbing rich kid would pay a nice ransom for those.

Then he renamed the file *Microsoft Document Help Guide*. He selected all of the text and changed it to a dingbat font so it would be impossible to do a simple keyword search for its contents, then stuck the whole thing in the Applications folder. Perfect.

Teachers were such dorks about computers. Glover would pop in an old *MythBusters* DVD for the class to watch while he looked for the file, which would take him most of the period. More likely, he'd have to call in the district tech guy, but no way would he bring in administrators or any security. Too embarrassing. Eventually he'd get it figured out and do the lab next week. He'd assume it was some virus. No harm, no foul.

Nick was about to log off when he spotted Glover's grade-book program. He clicked on fifth period and changed Burger's midterm grade from a D to a C-minus. A small enough change for Glover not to notice, hopefully, but Nick knew it would mean a lot to Burger's mom.

Nick logged off and peeked into the hallway. Burger

was lying flat on his back, half of his bulk hanging off the bench. His eyes were closed and his legs twitched like a big yellow Labrador dreaming about running.

"You know, narcolepsy is not really a desirable trait in a lookout," Nick said.

Burger, eyes still closed, let out a huge yawn. "What's narco-leprosy?"

"Falling asleep in the middle of the day. Could be a sign you've finally lost it. Seriously, Burger, someone could have come down the hall at any time."

Burger reached up and flicked at an earlobe. "No worries, dude. I got ears like a hawk."

Nick shook his head. "Come on. I'll buy you some pizza for being such a loyal watchdog."

"Nice!" Burger was up and through the doors like a shot. Nick was always surprised at how quickly Burger could move when he was motivated.

Nick said, "Let's see if we can make any more cash in this place before it's time to go home."

3

AFTER SCHOOL, NICK AND BURGER WERE MAKING
their way to the bike racks when they were knocked to
the ground by a rampaging wheelchair.

"Hey, watch it!" Burger ended up on his hands and
knees in a pile of scattered books and papers.

Chet Millard, a high schooler, worked the controls on
both armrests. His sleek wheelchair spun around, then
zipped right back to where Nick and Burger were picking
themselves up off the ground.

Custom-made in Italy by a famous racing firm, that
chair could go zero-to-cheetah-sprint in 4.3 seconds. Nick
had seen Chet pass the school bus on a dead straight-
away on that thing before. It probably cost more than

Nick's mom made in a year working at both the mill and the Hungry Lumberjack.

Chet twisted a dial and his seat cushion shot up on hydraulics until he was looking down at the boys. "Oh, so sorry, fellas. Just put in a new V-4 in this beauty, and I guess she got away from me." He proudly patted the side of his superchair with a thickly muscled arm.

Chet's legs may have been withered and lifeless, but he made up for it in upper-body strength. His parents had donated a pile of money so that the school could build a weight room to rival the Seattle Seahawks' training facility. Nick knew that Chet had his own key and basically lived in there. That tight black T-shirt clung to his bulging biceps like someone dangling off the edge of a cliff.

Chet looked down at Burger's scattered papers. "I'd help you clean up, my man, but I'm pretty busy." He inclined his head in the direction of a shiny silver Cadillac Escalade in the parking lot. "I need to go sit over there and wait for my friends."

"Watch where you're going next time." Burger scowled and dropped to one knee to pick up his stuff. "That chair should come with external airbags if you don't know how to steer it," he added, half under his breath.

Nick shook his head at his friend. Couldn't Burger just leave it alone?

Chet stopped backing up. His eyes narrowed. He eased his chair forward, the tires rolling to a rest on top of

Burger's notes. "Nobody talks about my chair. Besides, I've got better things to do than watch out for a couple of Smoke Valley lifers."

Burger's cheeks went all purple. He stood up and balled his hands into fists, but Nick grabbed his arm to restrain him. Getting into a public fight with Chet would be very bad. Not because he was in a wheelchair. Because they would lose.

"Come on, Chet, leave them alone." Hayley Millard approached from the back doors, throwing Nick a glance. "Sorry about my big brother." She rolled her eyes. "He's a little overly proud of Hell on Wheels there."

"No problem," Nick mumbled.

The doors to the gym burst open and a half-dozen guys sauntered out, headed straight for them. Big and burly, they wore letterman's jackets, branding them as football players for Bayside High. Chet looked from the jocks to the middle schoolers in front of him and back again. He spoke up when the group got within earshot.

"Actually, I think your friend here wants a problem." Chet yanked up the hand brake, then slammed the joystick on the armrest forward. The oversize tires with thick treads—more monster truck than conventional wheelchair—spun in place, ripping up some of Burger's papers and smoking against the asphalt. Chet slowly put his hand back on the brake's handle, grinning at the boys. If he let go, that souped-up machine would blast off, running right through them.

Nick sidestepped out of the way, but Burger stayed where he was, stubbornly playing chicken.

The football players formed a semicircle off to the side, watching the show.

Chet grinned at them. Then, in a flash, he released the brake, practically leaving a patch of melted rubber on the cement. Burger dove out of the way, sprawling across the wet grass, but Chet had already jerked the handle back up. The chair only nudged forward a foot or two.

Chet raised his palms and shook his head in mock sadness. "Sorry, my man. I'm telling you, this new V-4 is really acting up. I need to get a handle on all of this power."

The football players laughed and bumped fists with Chet. They were good at that. Chet was their ticket to get into the weight room after school hours, and the parties he threw were the stuff of Bayside legend.

Nick helped Burger get up and collect his schoolwork for the second time and pulled him over to the bike racks. He had always been good at reading the odds, and he decided that any further interaction with these guys was guaranteed to end in a loss.

Chet spun his chair around and headed toward his Escalade, the jocks following close behind. "Let's go, Sis," he called over his shoulder to Hayley. "Mom says I gotta take you home."

"Hey, wait." Hayley looked back and forth between the SUV and Nick. "I really am sorry about my brother. He's —you know—just showing off for those guys."

"Whatever." Nick shrugged. There had been run-ins with Chet before, and the best thing was to just keep away from him. He definitely wanted his interaction with the Millard family to be with Hayley instead of her brother, so he tried to keep the conversation going. "Did everything work out in Science today?"

Hayley gave him that crooked smile again and nodded. "We watched TV while Glover spent all period hunched over his computer, muttering to himself. I've never heard a teacher swear like that before." She gave Nick an appraising look. "I don't know what you did, but you must be a talented guy."

Nick hoped his face wasn't getting red. Nobody had ever really called him a "guy" before. He'd always been a "boy." Maybe he looked different because he was getting older. And how cool was it that Hayley Millard of all people was the first one to notice his *guyness*?

He realized he should probably say something back. Man, why did normal conversation have to be so much more complicated than negotiations? Maybe he should try—

"Come on, Nick." Burger was by the racks, but Nick was suddenly very embarrassed to retrieve his bike. It was a hand-me-down from a cousin. A girl cousin. It had taken him two hours with a metal file to scratch off the "Racing Princess" logos all over the frame.

Burger had found his bike at the dump last summer. After three months of constant repairs, the thing was more baling wire and duct tape than actual metal and chrome.

Nick was about to walk away, pretend that that wasn't his bike at all, when—

"Sweet rides, gentlemen. You really got those all tricked out," Chet called from the center of his friends. He whistled in mock appreciation. "Wanna trade for this piece of crap?"

He pointed a little remote at the back of the Escalade. The back door swung open. He punched another button and loud music blared from the car speakers while a loading ramp unfolded itself and descended smoothly until it touched the ground.

Chet zipped his wheelchair onto the ramp, which lifted him into the car. He grabbed a series of custom-made handles in the ceiling to hoist himself out of the chair and he swung smoothly between the backseats and into the driver's seat. Nick knew they made specially equipped steering wheels so that people could operate the gas and brakes by hand.

His buddies piled into the vehicle. The tinted driver's window slid down. "Get in, Hayley."

Hayley gave Nick a little wave and walked over to the SUV. She was about to get in when Burger called out to her.

"See you at the party this weekend!"

Hayley turned and gave Nick a stricken look. Chet stuck his head out the window. "What? You can't invite those two. You know what Mom says about having animals in the house."

The football players laughed and jeered as a couple of half-full Coke cans shot out the open windows. They hit the bikes and exploded in a warm shower of sticky soda.

"Jeez!" Burger said, wiping the syrupy liquid off his pants. "Gross!"

"Get in, Hayley."

She mouthed *Sorry* again at Nick and climbed into the SUV. The Escalade's tires chirped against the pavement as it sped away from the school. Nick didn't wipe his face right away. He didn't want to give Chet and his friends the satisfaction of watching that in their rearview mirror.

But he was going to make sure that he and Burger found Chet's bedroom sometime during the big party. If Chet liked to soak things in warm soda, then Nick figured he'd find a few prized possessions in there and return the favor.

"Let's get away from here." Nick pedaled away from the school, Burger right behind. The clouds started to spit out a misty drizzle.

Burger shrugged. "At least the rain'll wash off the soda, huh?"

Nick didn't say anything.

Burger sped up until they were riding side by side. "So...you sure you don't feel like spending any of that money? They probably have a used copy of Zombie Golf at Reset Games by now. It'll be half price."

Nick shook his head. Sometimes he envied Burger's ability to immediately shake off crappy things that happened.

"I've heard that game's so awesome, though. If you take too long setting up your putt, the zombies converge and you have to fight your way to the next tee. You can use the putter to smash them in the brains!"

Nick remained silent, watching the suburban houses drift by as they pedaled. It was at times like these that he missed having his dad around the most. Someone to ask for advice on girls, or money, or whatever. Of course, if his dad had stuck around, Nick wouldn't have to be worrying about the money in the first place.

"Come on, dude. The golf carts have rear-mounted rocket launchers and spring-loaded chain saws. Maximum zombie carnage!" Burger made rocket-launching noises and chain saw–buzzing noises, followed by squelchy bodies-being-torn-apart noises. Then he laughed maniacally.

"Sounds fun. But you know I have to save the money."

Burger scoffed. "You don't need to buy the whole college, you know. You just need enough for tuition."

Nick remained quiet, wishing that he really were saving for college. That would sure make everything in his life a lot easier. Maybe someday.

The houses thinned out and were replaced by fir trees. The sidewalks ended as well, and he and Burger rode their bikes on the gravelly shoulder.

"You know what's going to happen if you go to a big, fancy college someday, right?"

"Shut it. We're not buying Zombie Golf."

"I'm being serious." Burger wiped the sweat from his eyes. "Someplace like that is just going to be filled with the same kind of rich kids who annoy you so much now. Like Chet and his lame friends. Why bother?"

Burger tore away, rode up a piece of plywood leaning against a rock, and jumped his bike off the end. He lifted one arm skyward while he was in the air and nearly botched the landing, but he managed to stay upright.

Nick sighed. He knew Burger was probably right, as weird as it felt to take advice from him. The truth was, Nick didn't exactly know what he wanted, other than not wanting to be the third Stringer generation of millworkers. He just knew he had to find something that he was good at, and that he actually liked to do. He didn't enjoy all of the hustling at school—his teachers were actually pretty nice to him—but he didn't feel like he had much of a choice. He hoped that someday—

"Race you home!" Burger yelled. The boys had left the city line behind them. There were no houses in sight, and they were approaching Chuckanut Drive, the long, swervy road cut into the side of Lookout Mountain, which towered over the bay.

Burger stood on his pedals and pumped furiously, the bike lunging from side to side. Nick followed with a burst of speed of his own. They were headed up an incline and he knew it was his only time to pull away. Once they crested the rise and headed downhill, Burger's extra poundage would transform from liability to asset. He coasted way faster than Nick.

Nick shot into the lead. Burger grabbed for Nick's sweatshirt—a move that would probably have resulted in both bikes crashing—but Nick lunged out of the way and Burger grasped at air.

Using a steady, measured pace, Nick increased his lead over Burger, who had temporarily exhausted himself with his crazed takeoff. The boys rounded a corner and got their first glimpse of the water over two hundred feet below.

The view was stunning, even on a day like this, when the sky was covered with dark clouds. The choppy expanse of the bay stretched as far as Nick could see, broken up only by the San Juan Islands, forested domes shrouded in fog.

Every summer some luxury car company hired a Hollywood film crew to fly up and shoot a commercial around here. Those new BMWs looked even better racing against the side of the cliff, hugging the outside white line, only a few feet of open air separating the new car from a fatal fall to the rocks jutting up below. Apparently these commercials appealed to middle-aged men who wanted to pretend they were the star of an action movie.

The road was freshly wet from the drizzle, the worst conditions for a race. It messed with the way the bike handled and limited the visibility of the people driving in cars.

But when Burger bellowed out a war whoop and drew closer, Nick raced on anyway. As usual. Sometimes it was fun to just turn off his brain and do stupid stuff with his best friend.

The road sloped downward. Nick glanced over his shoulder and saw Burger barreling toward him, working his pedals into a blur. His bulky frame made the bike look like one of those tiny novelties that clowns rode in parades. The wind and rain had turned Burger's blond hair into a flyaway mess, perfectly matching the demon grin plastered across his face. He looked like a crazy person.

"I will destroy you!" Burger yelled. Or something like that; it was hard for Nick to hear with his tires sluicing through the rainwater and the wind whistling by his ears.

In another minute Burger was almost right on top of Nick. Even though it was reckless, Nick let his bike drift toward the center line, cutting off Burger's passing lane. He kept an eye on the corner up ahead, making sure no cars were coming.

Burger lunged in the other direction, shoulders hunched over his front tire. Nick veered back into position, forcing Burger to clutch his brakes to avoid a collision.

Back and forth they went, Nick zigging and zagging to

maintain his lead. He bore down on the pedals and edged in front of Burger, angling back toward the center stripe. A long, straight stretch of empty road opened up before the next corner and he needed to create some distance from both Burger and the suicidal fall off the cliff.

Then a flash of purple light sparked in front of him. He only had a second to register that the light formed a huge circle—like the entrance to a tunnel, almost—before he saw three things all at once:

1. A big delivery truck was suddenly in the middle of the road.
2. A bear was driving it.
3. The front grille was going to smash into his bike in two seconds.

4

NICK DID A FULL-BODY CRINGE AND LAID THE BIKE down on the slick pavement. His right leg scraped along the road, pinned beneath him.

The truck swerved so quickly it leaned over sideways, up on two wheels. Then it smashed through the guardrail —the metal screaming in protest—plunged over the cliff, and dropped out of sight.

Burger's front tire plowed into Nick's bike and he went sprawling over his handlebars onto the asphalt. The boys lay dazed in a jumbled heap.

Burger lumbered to his feet first. Rainwater mixed with blood from a cut on his cheek, making him look like something from a horror movie. He staggered to the cliff's edge.

The cuff of Nick's jeans was caught in the bike chain, and he disentangled himself while Burger paced along the ledge, swiveling his head back and forth.

Nick's relief at being alive was quickly swallowed up by the dread twisting his stomach. It was totally their fault that truck had gone over the edge. Could anyone have survived a crash like that? Because what he saw in the driver's seat had to be a hallucination, there was no way that a—

"That was insane!" Burger wiped his bloodied face with the sleeve of his jacket. "Seriously, where did it come from? One second: not there. Next second: totally there!"

"What?" Nick struggled to stand up, his thoughts as foggy as the hidden islands out in the bay. Had all of that really just happened? There was a gaping hole in the guardrail, metal twisted out of shape on each side, so he couldn't have dreamed it.

He could hardly believe he was still alive. That truck had missed his front tire by maybe an inch or two.

Nick limped over to Burger, wincing at the pain in his road rash–covered leg. He peered over the edge. It was a sheer, rocky drop-off for a good fifty feet, and after that the slope grew gradually less steep. The gentler incline sprouted bushes and trees, growing thicker and thicker down the hill until a dense copse of woods blocked the view of the water's edge, far below. There was a hole punched through the canopy of branches, but he didn't see any truck.

"We have to get down there. Someone's going to need our help, bad." Burger clamped his hands to either side of his head, as if trying to keep his scrambled brains from leaking right out his ears from the shock of it all. "Hey— you saw it appear all of a sudden, too, right? I mean, I'm not *that* crazy."

Nick rubbed at his temples, trying to focus. "The truck?"

"Of course, the truck!" Burger threw his hands in the air. "The one that appeared out of nowhere? Almost steamrolled us?"

Nick tried to freeze that bizarre split second of memory in his mind. If Burger had seen it, too, then maybe Nick wasn't going totally bonkers. "I thought maybe you meant the...you know, the..."

Burger made a broad *keep-it-going* gesture with both arms. "The *what*? There was something more amazing than a truck appearing out of nothingness?" He looked at Nick and his face softened. "Dude. Are you okay? You look ...I don't know, even worse than someone who almost got creamed by a ghost truck."

Nick couldn't believe he was going to say it out loud. "I could have sworn there was a bear in the driver's seat."

Burger stared at Nick for a long moment, then looked back and forth between him and the bottom of the cliff.

"You believe me, right?" Nick was definitely not used to verifying his mental state by using Burger as a barometer for normal.

"Of course. It's you." Burger took another look over the ledge. "Besides, a truck just appeared out of the air. I'd believe that a two-headed shark in a tuxedo was riding shotgun."

Nick nodded. "We need to get down there." He climbed on his bike and Burger followed.

Nick pedaled along the narrow shoulder while Burger brought up the rear. They hardly watched the road, instead peering down at the forest below, searching the thickets of woods they had been exploring ever since fourth grade.

"You think it made it all the way to the trees?" Burger said. "Looks like it was headed for our fort."

"I guess," Nick said. "Or else...do you think maybe it could have just disappeared as fast as it showed up?"

"I'd believe that, too."

Nick nodded. "Man, I hope so."

"Seriously?"

"Of course. Do you really want to be responsible for a fatal crash?"

"Good point. Let's get down there and figure this out."

They cruised for half a mile, leaving the sheer cliff wall behind for a spot where the drop-off was much less severe. Here the forest reached up the hill almost to the roadside.

The boys pulled off onto the shoulder and then coasted down a grassy incline to the dense thicket of underbrush on the outskirts of the woods. They jumped off their bikes and pushed aside a screen of fern fronds to reveal a narrow opening between two big rocks. A hidden trail.

Nick put up a hand, stopping Burger. "Wait. What about 911?" The short ride had cleared his head. He felt more like himself.

Burger looked uneasy. "Is this really something you want to get the police involved with? Before we even know what's going on? They're gonna ask us what we were doing."

"But what if somebody's hurt down there?"

"We don't even know if it was real yet."

"Then what was it?"

"I don't know. A hologram or something?" Burger spread his arms wide. "Real trucks don't just pop up in the middle of the road. Especially driven by, you know..."

Nick was glad Burger didn't actually mention the bear again. He was already talking himself back into believing that it must have been some panic-induced hallucination.

He bit his lip and looked up at the highway, then back at Burger. "I don't know. I still think we should call."

"Look, you're scared. Totally understandable, dude. But that doesn't mean—"

"I'm not *scared*."

"Freaked out, then. Whatever."

Nick glanced back at the road, drumming his fingers on the handlebars. He didn't like relying on Burger for major decisions. But this was all happening so fast....

Burger cleared his throat and stepped closer, lowering

his voice even though they were very alone. "Okay. Not gonna lie, Nick. When that truck appeared and almost hit us . . . a tiny bit of pee squirted out. Tell anyone and I'll kill you, obviously. Just wanted to let you know you weren't the only one a little spooked around here."

Nick set his shoulders and pushed on his handlebars. "I'm not *spooked*, either." But he was lying. Nick liked to know all the angles before he made a bet, and there was no way to lay odds on such an impossibly messed-up situation. "Fine. Let's go."

5

THE BIG DELIVERY TRUCK LAY ON ITS SIDE LIKE A wounded animal, half buried in a thicket of blackberry brambles.

But other than that—somehow—it looked okay. The wheels hadn't been torn off, the sides weren't all smashed in. Even the windshield was still intact.

The boys were hiding behind a big Douglas fir, peeking around the trunk to watch for any signs of movement.

"It looks pretty real," Burger whispered. "But I have no idea how it's still in one piece."

"I hope the same is true for whoever's in there." Nick gulped. "Or *what*ever's in there."

The truck's dirty white side panels were bare of any corporate logos or slogans. The back end was a tall, windowless rectangle, like on a UPS truck. But this vehicle looked old-fashioned; with its white-walled front tires it reminded Nick of one of those milk delivery trucks from black-and-white movies.

And it seemed so out of place in the middle of the woods. *Their* woods. This area, not accessible by any road, had always been his and Burger's private playground for exploring. No parents or teachers were ever down here to tell them what to do.

The rain had let up but was still dripping from the pine needles. It splashed down on Nick and he wiped his forehead. "So we need some kind of plan. First we should—"

But Burger was already striding toward the sideways truck. He could always be counted on to act first and think later. Nick followed, still more than a little wary, as his friend hoisted himself up on top of the front tire, then crawled along the passenger-side door. He leaned forward and peeked in the window.

"See anything?" Nick said from below. "Is there any ...you know..." He couldn't bring himself to describe the blood-and-guts milk shake he imagined splattered all over the inside of the cab. With maybe some fur poking out.

Burger dropped back down and shook his head. "Nothing. No one there."

For Nick, the relief felt like shrugging off a backpack full of rocks. They hadn't killed anybody. It cleared his mind; time to figure out what was going on here.

"Hello? Hello!" Nick turned a slow circle in the clearing, cupping his hands around his mouth and shouting into the woods. "Anybody out there?"

"Are you hurt?" Burger shouted.

Nick scanned the grass around the truck, looking for a telltale trail of blood leading off into the forest. Nothing.

"Okay, let's find out what's in the back of this thing." Nick turned and made his way to the rear of the truck. Burger joined him.

Nick took a deep breath and grabbed the handle on the loading door. He couldn't get the image of the bear staring at him through the windshield out of his mind. Maybe the weirdest part—the part that made him think it couldn't be a hallucination—was that the bear had looked as surprised as Nick had been. He tried to push the image from his mind.

Burger wedged in beside him, clearly eager to see what the truck held in store.

Eeerch! Nick forced open one of the door panels on rusty hinges.

A head fell out the back of the truck.

"AAAAGHGHGH!"

Burger's feet skitter-danced backward, knocking Nick over and sending them both thudding to the ground. The tangled-up boys frantically tried to get away, looking like a four-legged beast scrambling in the mud. Finally they separated, several yards away from the truck, panting heavily.

"Gross," Nick breathed.

"Totally." Burger gestured toward the head. "But at least now we know the driver wasn't a bear, huh?"

Nick gagged and put a hand over his mouth. He staggered back a few more steps.

"Hey, wait up," Burger called. "I'm just kidding." Nick watched as his friend approached the truck. What was he thinking?

"Stay away from there. We have to get help and try to—"

"No, look!" Burger grabbed the head by its black hair and held it up. Nick fought the gag reflex again and nearly lost. "It's just a mask!"

Nick really looked at it for the first time. Burger was right. The rubber face dangled from his grasp, cheeks sunken in and eyeholes staring blankly up at the trees. There were scars crisscrossed into the face, and the whole thing had a greenish tint. Maybe it was supposed to be a Frankenstein's monster mask.

"That's really weird," Nick said.

"It gets better. Come here."

Burger kicked open the other door and spread out before them was a jumble of costumes, tossed all over the interior in the wreck.

Lying just inside the door was a full suit of medieval-style armor, the iron fingers of its gloves wrapped around the pommel of a great sword. The breastplate even had authentic-looking dents and scratches scored into the surface, as if the armor had seen some heavy battle action.

Draped over the medieval knight was a dragon costume so large that it must have been meant for two or more people. The scaly tail coiled around the feet of the suit of armor while the ferocious head stared at the boys.

"That thing looks hungry," Burger said.

The pile of costumes was deep. There were stacks and stacks of garment boxes, but dozens of them had burst open and spilled costumes everywhere. Nick could see bits of a mummy poking out next to the dragon, its wrappings frayed and discolored to appear ancient. Then he caught glimpses of a werewolf, a zombie with a half-eaten face, a hook-nosed witch with hairy moles all over her face, and some kind of purplish squid-monster.

"I wonder what this is all about," said Nick.

"Who knows? Solves your mystery about the driver, though."

"What do you mean?"

Burger gestured at the costumes. "Must have had a bear costume up front with him. Sitting in the passenger's seat for a joke or something."

"Maybe..." He reached forward and rubbed a dragon scale between his fingers. "Man, these things are so realistic."

Nick's inner cash register started to work overtime. These costumes had to be worth a lot of money. Thousands, probably. Heck, he knew a rental place in town that charged over a hundred bucks for the use of outfits like these just for a single weekend. He sized up the storage area and figured there might be fifty costumes in here, maybe more. The numbers and dollar signs swirled in his head: fifty costumes multiplied by, say, two thousand dollars each, plus the—

"Nick." The word came out in a choked whisper. "Turn. Around. Slooow-ly."

"What now?"

Nick turned. Burger was staring into the forest, his mouth gaping comically wide. Nick stepped away from the truck and froze.

About thirty yards away, a seven-foot-tall grizzly bear was up on his hind legs. He was facing away from the boys, standing in front of an elm tree. They could hear a stream of liquid splashing against the bark.

"Is that bear really . . . you know . . . ?" Burger whispered.

Nick nodded again.

The bear was peeing on the tree, standing straight up like he was at a urinal in the men's room.

"I didn't know they did it like that," Burger whispered.

"I don't think they do."

The bear let out a satisfied growl-sigh and reached around with a big paw to scratch at his furry rump.

Nick took a careful backward step. "We have to get out of here."

The grizzly pushed away from the tree and took a few shaky steps before dropping clumsily to all fours.

He was shuffling in the direction of the truck when he saw the boys.

He tilted his shaggy head on massive shoulders, studying Nick and Burger with the confused look of a dog that can't find the ball you just threw for him.

"What should we do?" Burger's voice was a husky whisper. It sounded more like a plea to the gods than an actual question for his friend.

The bear climbed back up on unsteady hind legs. While he was trying to gain his balance he held a paw up in the air in what seemed to Nick—impossibly—like the *just-give-me-one-minute-here-and-I'll-be-right-with-you* gesture.

Then the bear looked straight at the boys, raised his head to the sky, and clawed at his throat with both paws. He did it slowly, with deliberate care, but that just made the whole scene even creepier.

Finally the bear dropped back down to all fours and regarded the boys again.

"*Roar?*"

It was a very un-bearlike sound. But it was enough to break the boys' paralysis.

"Run!" Burger yelled, his thick legs working like pistons.

Nick took off after him, pushing fern fronds out of his way and jumping over fallen branches. After a minute he glanced over his shoulder, expecting his entire field of vision to be filled with jaws and teeth.

43

But as the bear lumbered after Nick, his front paws hit a soft spot. He slipped and did a face-plant in the mud. Nick had never seen such a klutzy animal.

That didn't lessen his terror, however. Nick faced forward and bolted after his friend.

And that's when he noticed that Burger had a garment box clutched underneath each of his meaty arms.

6

THE BOYS SAT ON THE STEPS OF BURGER'S BACK-
yard deck, still panting from breaking the world land
speed record climbing up the hill and racing home.

"Do you feel bad that we just took off like that?" Burger
said.

"The charging wild animal didn't leave us a lot of
choice."

"But what if the bear finds the driver?"

"I already told you. I think the bear *was* the driver."
Nick shook his head. "But that still doesn't make any
sense, does it?"

"It's been the craziest day ever."

"I know. First that truck appears out of nowhere, and

then it's not even scratched after it falls off the cliff, and then—"

"No, I was talking about Hayley Millard smiling at you. I never thought I'd see that in my life." Burger grinned. "That was way weirder than the magical truck and the driving bear and all the costumes."

Nick tried to punch Burger in the shoulder, but Burger had jumped up to grab the garment boxes.

Burger opened them and spread out the costumes on the grass. The nearest house besides Nick's was a quarter mile down the Lost Meadows Road, so they weren't worried about anyone seeing them.

One of the costumes was a full-size gorilla suit and the other was some kind of a robot. Even on the ground they looked just as realistic as everything else back in that truck.

"Whoa," Nick said.

Burger grinned. "Totally."

Nick knelt and took one of the gorilla's hands in his own and ran his fingers along the palm. What kind of material had been used to make this look so convincing? The black palm was smooth in some parts and callused in others, with deep lines embedded in the surface just like a real hand. Or paw. Whatever.

Burger dropped down beside him, grabbed the gorilla's leathery ear, and propped up the head. The details of the scowling face were hideously perfect. "So, Mr. Vocabulary.

Whaddaya call it when they stuff dead animals, make it look like they're still alive and stuff?"

"Taxidermy."

"Right. This looks more like taxidermy than a costume."

"I know. It even *smells* like a gorilla," Nick said.

"How would you know what a gorilla smells like?"

"I've been hanging out with you since kindergarten."

"Real funny."

They stood back up, arms crossed over their chests while they studied the other costume.

Burger gave Nick a sideways glance. "You're not mad at me or anything, are you?"

"For what?"

"You know. *Borrowing* the costumes?" Burger cleared his throat. "It's kinda hard sometimes to figure out where you stand on rules, you know? Some you break, some you don't."

Nick shrugged. "I figured you were just protecting them from that bear. Right?"

"Good point." Burger nodded. "He would have ripped these to shreds."

"Or peed all over them."

That got a laugh from Burger. "So what are we gonna do with them now?"

Nick sighed. "I suppose we will have to return them. Try to find some contact information in the truck if that bear clears out of the area." He was no thief. Sure, he made his money at school, but that was for providing legitimate services to paying customers. Besides, there would probably be a nice finder's fee for helping to get those costumes back to whoever owned them.

"Yeah, I guess you're right," Burger said, clearly disappointed.

Nick shrugged. "We'll probably have to wait until Monday, though. You know, regular business hours and all that."

Burger perked up. "So until then, maybe a gorilla and a droid could crash Hayley's fancy party tomorrow?"

"I think it's appropriate to give these things a field test."

"Nice! Man, I was hoping you'd say that. Just think about it—we're gonna have the best costumes at a Bay-view Gardens party!" Burger pointed at the robot. "But that one kinda looks more like the Tin Woodman than a real droid," he said. "You know, from *The Wizard of Oz*?"

"Yeah, it's a little clunky. Like a robot in those old-timey sci-fi movies." Nick knelt again and ran his finger-tips along the metallic plates of the costume's body. "But it's still pretty amazing."

Jax, Burger's golden retriever, circled the costumes warily. Every now and then he would dart in for a sniff of gorilla fur, then scamper back out of reach.

"It seems like these'd be too expensive to just sell for Halloween. Maybe they were headed to one of those movie studios up in Vancouver?" Nick continued to study the costumes. "That would explain the bear, right? Someone was delivering a bear and a bunch of costumes for some film shoot up there?"

Burger nodded. "Oh, yeah. I like where you're going with that." A smile spread across his face. "You must be thinking what I'm thinking, right?"

"I always hope not."

Burger made the touchdown sign with both arms over his head. "Movie Fight!"

Nick rolled his eyes. Movie Fight was Burger's favorite game: staging elaborate combat sequences to rival the good-guy-finally-meets-the-big-boss scenes at the end of every action movie.

But without stuntmen and professional choreographers, their backyard brawls were a little more dangerous. (The main problem was usually Burger forgetting that not everyone weighed more than two hundred pounds in the seventh grade.) One time they both threw punches at the exact same moment and their fists had smashed together. Nick hadn't been able to use his right hand for two weeks. And they had both agreed to never mention the slippery roof incident again.

"Don't you remember last time? The epic 'sword fight'?"

"Oh, come on," Burger said. "That sharp stick didn't actually touch the *ball* part of your eyeball. Just the part right under the socket."

"Maybe you remember the stitches?"

"You only needed eight."

"Right. One stitch for every week that I was grounded afterward."

"You have to admit: it was all worth it for the ambulance ride." Burger swooped around the yard, making an *eee-ooo-eee-oooo* siren noise and mimicking the way the ambulance had torn around the twists and turns of Chuckanut Drive.

It was one of the few times Nick had seen his mom furious. Without health insurance, an ambulance ride was really expensive. "Forget it. I've had enough near-death experiences for one morning, thanks."

"This'll be different."

"They're going to write that on your tombstone, you know."

As Burger circled the yard again, he scooped up the robot's metallic helmet. "No, seriously. Look, this thing will be like armor." He picked up a stick and smacked the faceplate a few times. The stick plinked harmlessly against the surface. "See? Little Nicky will be so safe and comfy inside there."

"Don't call me that." Nick picked up the robot costume. It *would* be pretty fun to have a reason to try these on. "I guess it wouldn't hurt to at least see how they fit before the big party."

"Awesome!" Burger picked up the gorilla. "Does that mean we get to put these on and smash into each other now?"

"Fine. But I'm not sure you're going to be able to walk around in that thing. It's huge, even for you."

But Burger already had one leg in the costume and was hopping around, trying to jam the other one in while he pulled on the zipper that ran down the middle of the gorilla.

Nick rolled his eyes again and slipped an arm into the silver sleeve of the robot costume. He struggled with the chest plate, trying to find where the clasps fit together, and—

"RO-OOAA-AARRGGGH!"

Nick dropped the robot and spun around.

Yikes. The costume looked even more realistic now that Burger had it on. Could it have expanded, somehow? It didn't seem possible that Burger—even as big as he was—could be filling out the whole thing. And that roar. The mask must have come with a hidden megaphone or speaker or something.

Gorilla-Burger looked down at his costume. He slowly raised one black palm in front of his face and wiggled his fingers. Then he moved closer to Nick in that way great apes walk, knuckles pressed into the ground for stability and legs swing-shuffling beneath him. It was eerie, how natural it looked. He covered ground quickly.

Jax was on full alert: head lowered, haunches raised, and growling from deep in his throat. Nick stepped backward. "You're kind of freaking me out, Burger."

Gorilla-Burger stopped, opened his mouth, and a

series of guttural grunts and primal screeches came out. "Ooh eee ungh ahhgh EEEECH." He tilted his head and carefully raised massive fingers to his face to feel the dark lips there. Then he collected a deep breath, massive pectoral muscles expanding, and spoke again, but more of the same came out. "Ah ergh eeech agh ooh."

Then Nick saw the genuinely baffled expression in his eyes. Was Burger *scared?*

Nick could certainly understand if he was. It was so creepy—those eyes looked very human and totally out of place in that shaggy head.

"Burger, is that"—the question seemed as ridiculous as the one about the bear driving the truck—"is that *you* in there?"

Gorilla-Burger slowly lifted a hairy arm and gave Nick a thumbs-up. "Agh ooh eep urg," he grunted. He clapped a hand over his mouth and shook his head fiercely.

"Burger. You—this costume—it's all so..." Nick took a deep breath. "Burger, you look like a real gorilla. Even more than usual."

Then Nick saw something change in Gorilla-Burger's eyes. A flicker of realization, followed by a very familiar look: Burger's wide-eyed enthusiasm.

Suddenly Burger the beast sprang into action. He raced across the backyard in that fluid ape-shamble, headed for the wooden jungle gym.

Jax shot across the lawn, lunging for the beast's heels, intent on defending his backyard supremacy. Just as the dog closed in, his teeth inches from clamping down on black fur, Gorilla-Burger launched himself into the air. He grabbed one of the chains attached to a swing and shinnied hand over hand until he reached the top beam. Then he hoisted himself up and did a flip with the liquid grace of an Olympic gymnast, until he was standing on top of the jungle gym, over fifteen feet off the ground.

Nick noticed that his ape feet gripped the beam like a pair of hands. Gorilla-Burger raced along the length of it with scary good balance. When he reached the end, he vaulted into the air again, soaring so far that he landed on top of the carport, an impossible distance away. The plywood roof bowed under his weight.

He dashed across the top of the carport, then leapt onto the house, grabbing on to a second-story window-sill. He scaled the house, a black-haired blur, swinging back and forth. Gorilla-Burger gripped window ledges and chimney stones with both hands and feet for support. Finally he reached the roof and flipped up so that he was standing right on the edge, toes in the gutter, towering above the yard below. He roared. Jax scampered into his doghouse and hid under a blanket.

Gorilla-Burger beat his chest and bellowed at the sky. Then he looked down at Nick, panting and snorting.

There is no way this could be happening, thought Nick. But he couldn't deny the muddy footprints all over the side of the house, or the ape-slobber that was dripping down to splatter on the porch.

"Man, that is so much better than your usual gorilla impersonation," Nick called.

Gorilla-Burger turned and jumped off the roof backward. Nick's breath caught in his throat—a stunt like that should have been suicide—but Burger caught the corner of the wall, straddle-gripping both sides with hands and feet, and slid down to the grass.

Nick stood perfectly still while Gorilla-Burger loped toward him. The beast came right up to him, then settled back on his haunches and snorted loudly. His huge nostrils were jet black and crinkly, and steam rose out of them as he snorted again.

Nick studied that furry face for a moment. "So...you really can't talk in there?"

Gorilla-Burger shook his head.

Nick exhaled a long and shaky breath. "I have no idea what's going on, but at least that's a bonus."

Gorilla-Burger growled menacingly and puffed out his enormous chest. Nick stumbled backward a few steps. Burger stopped growling and spread his lips apart, revealing all of his teeth. But Nick thought maybe it was more smile than grimace.

Gorilla-Burger bent over, collected the robot costume in both hands, and held it out to Nick. He grunted encouragingly.

"I don't understand any of this." Nick looked down at the costume and then up at Gorilla-Burger. "Do you?"

The beast shrugged his giant shoulders.

"Look, this is weird. I can admit now that I'm pretty freaked out. What about you?" Nick paused, cleared his throat. "You spooked?"

Gorilla-Burger held his palms an inch apart.

"Come on."

He moved his hands until they were three feet apart.

"Uh-huh. But I bet you still want me to put this thing on, right?"

"Aaagh eep ooop aarp *EEEE!*" Big grimace-smile.

Nick grinned back. It might be kind of fun to be inside a real robot for a little while. What was the worst that could happen?

7

NICK DIDN'T FEEL NUMB IN THE ROBOT SUIT, exactly. More like his mind had been detached from his body.

Was this the way the world really looked? In perfect resolution and high definition, each color so rich it dazzled, the edge of every object this sharply defined?

And seriously, how could all of this even be happening, anyway?

A flicker of motion in a clump of ferns about a dozen yards away caught his attention.

A thought came to him. But it didn't seem like a normal thought, more like a suggestion:

ZOOM IN?

Sure. It'd be cool to be able to zoom in like a camera and see what was—

Suddenly his field of vision rushed forward until all he could see was a single fern frond in perfect clarity. And there on the green surface was a ladybug, a big one, wiggling around.

No, wait, it only looked so large because it was actually two ladybugs, sort of stuck together, and they were ...oh, wow...they were in the middle of making more ladybugs.

Zoom out! Quick! Zoom out! Again, this didn't feel like a thought. More like a command he was giving his eyes.

His field of vision pulled back to reveal the entire backyard. Phew. If his senses were going to be this sharp, he was going to have to be a little more careful where he looked.

An idea came to him. He craned his neck back on metallic joints to look up at the sky. The pale form of the moon was just visible in the late-afternoon sky.

TELESCOPIC ZOOM?

Oh, totally.

His field of vision rushed forward again, and suddenly he could make out the jagged edges of individual craters on the lunar surface. The details looked like something out of one of his science textbooks. What kind of a costume came equipped with a telescope lens in the eyeholes?

His attention came rushing back to the yard when Gorilla-Burger leaned forward and jabbed him in the chest plate with a finger as thick as a bratwurst. It seemed like it should have knocked him off his feet, but Nick just stood there like a statue.

Could he even move? He gave a thought command to his legs and they instantly churned beneath him. He passed right by Gorilla-Burger. Nick watched the reflection from the sliding-glass door on the back porch: a metallic-silver droid marching across the backyard. Surreal, but so cool. Even better than movie special effects. Wait—that must be it. These weren't movie costumes, they were movie *props*. That's why they were able to—

Clank! He ran into one of the jungle gym's wooden posts. Gorilla-Burger pointed and screeched out a burst of monkey laughter.

Robo-Nick commanded himself to back up and turn around. He marched again, turning just in time to avoid crashing into the playhouse that belonged to Burger's little sisters.

After a few minutes of practice he was able to put the commands on autopilot, shifting directions and varying speed with the slightest thought. He started to feel like his whole self was on autopilot.

He snuck another peek in the window's reflection, but the sensors on the back of his helmet instantly went hot and a message flashed through his mind:

WARNING! IMMINENT DANGER OF—

And that's when four hundreds pounds of gorilla slammed into his back, driving him face-first into the grass.

Nick commanded himself to roll over, and Gorilla-Burger pounced on top of him. Nick distantly realized that he should feel crushed, but he only registered a slight pressure on his midsection.

Gorilla-Burger sat on Nick's chest plate and put his furry knees on top of the metal arms, pinning them to the lawn. When he leaned over, black fur and white teeth filled Nick's field of vision.

Gorilla-Burger slowly raised one thick finger. He let it hover in the air for a moment...and then *thunked* Nick in the forehead. The classic big-brother torture technique made an echoey clang against metal. Gorilla-Burger raised the finger again...and gave Nick another *thunk* between the eyes. Nick struggled to get free, but Gorilla-Burger was way too heavy. He grimace-smiled and bobbed his head up and down. "Eee ooh ooh ee *EEE!*" Another *thunk*. More primate giggling.

Nick was starting to remember (*thunk!*) that he had vowed never again to play (*thunk!*) Movie Fight with Burger under any (*thunk!*) circumstances, because his idiot friend never knew (*thunk!*) when to quit.

Nick stopped struggling; it was useless. Hopefully Burger would get bored soon, and then—

GENERATE ENEMY-ELECTROCUTING
FORCE FIELD?

Well, well...what a great suggestion. But he didn't want to kill Burger. Right?

He was dimly aware that it was getting harder to think for himself. As himself. On some level he knew that he would definitely be sad if Burger wasn't there anymore. But it was difficult to remember what sad felt like.

Thunk! Thunk!

A message kept overriding his thoughts, like a prime directive: an enemy was threatening him and needed to be disabled.

> SETTINGS:
> WARN
> STUN
> INCAPACITATE
> TERMINATE
> INCINERATE

Acceptable. He could eliminate the threat without lethal force. Nick mentally selected the STUN command. Bzzzzt! He felt a tremor as the electrical current shot throughout the casing of his torso.

Gorilla-Burger sat straight up and his eyes went wide. "Urk?"

He jumped off Nick and hopped around the yard, clutching his monkey butt in both hands and squealing.

Nick commanded himself to stand up. "HA. HA. HA. HA. HA." It came out tinny and stilted, like those computer voice programs. Felt more like an actor reading lines than actual laughter.

"RO-OARR-ARGHH!"

Gorilla-Burger had climbed on top of the playhouse. He beat his chest and bared his teeth, fiercely this time. Something had changed in his eyes. They looked wilder. The beast pointed at Nick, hunched his shoulders, and leaned forward, ready to attack.

Nick raised both hands and motioned the metallic fingers toward himself a few times: *Come and get it.*

Gorilla-Burger leapt off the playhouse, snarling. Nick retreated, maintaining a safe distance. Beast and machine circled each other in the center of the lawn.

Suddenly Gorilla-Burger charged Nick and swung a hairy arm at his head. Nick commanded his silver elbow to rise up and block it. *Clang!* Gorilla-Burger retreated, howling in pain.

Gorilla-Burger lunged and swung again. *Clang!* He snarled. The beast feinted ... then withdrew ... feinted ... withdrew ... but Nick was getting the hang of these robot commands—or perhaps the robot was getting the hang of him—and every attack was easily rebuffed.

Gorilla-Burger raised both arms to beat at his chest

and lifted his head to roar at the sky, leaving his abdomen exposed. *Time to go on the offensive.* Nick bent in half, aiming his metal helmet, and launched himself forward like a torpedo. He caught Gorilla-Burger in the solar plexus.

"Oof!" The air rushed out of the hairy beast. Gorilla-Burger fell back on his haunches, gripping his stomach.

Nick closed in for another assault, but Gorilla-Burger scrambled back up and loped away. *Is he quitting already?* Nick thought. *It would be unfortunate if he were badly hurt.*

But as soon as he thought it, the idea seemed strange. It was only a flesh-and-blood creature, after all. Organic beings got "hurt" all the time. It was one of the biggest disadvantages of not being a product of precise and efficient engineering.

But it turned out the creature was not quitting, merely devising a simple strategy. Gorilla-Burger grabbed a tire swing and pulled, straining his enormous shoulders, until the thick rope that attached it to the maple tree snapped as easily as an old rubber band. Then he ran at Nick, gripping the tire in both hands like an oversize discus. Gorilla-Burger planted his feet, twisted his torso, and heaved the tire. It flew in a direct path toward Nick's head. These illogical beasts were so barbaric, even a step below the humans.

INCOMING FOREIGN OBJECT DETECTED.
ENGAGE LASER CANNON?

Indeed.

Nick saw a thick red beam of light shoot out from his helmet. When it struck, the tire dissolved in midair. Black globules of melted rubber splattered the grass harmlessly at Nick's metallic feet.

Gorilla-Burger curled his black upper lip into a sneer. His eyes scanned the yard. Nick watched as he raced to the side of the house and set his huge fingers to fumbling with an exterior spigot. Gorilla-Burger grabbed a bucket and started filling it up.

Unacceptable. Water and electronics were not a good mix.

Gorilla-Burger picked up the bucket and charged. Nick commanded his legs to zig and zag him around the yard, but Gorilla-Burger closed in fast. Nick circled around the jungle gym, then dashed behind the playhouse for cover, but to no avail.

EVASIVE MEASURES DETECTED. ENGAGE ROCKET BOOSTERS?

A roar erupted directly behind him. Nick chanced a look over his shoulder and saw the bucket, held high and ready for dousing. Nick felt a bit more like himself as a degree of panic leaked into his artificially calm mind.

Yes! Engage rocket boosters! Now!

He shot straight up into the air as the water hit the

grass where his body had been a second before. Gorilla-Burger howled in frustration.

Nick soared. He instinctively leaned forward and zoomed smoothly over the top of the playhouse. He spread his arms out and tilted his shoulders and torso, pulling his flight path into a perfect circle over the backyard.

Gorilla-Burger shook a furry fist at him. Nick waved as he flew by, calculating that it would anger the irrational creature.

Time to experiment. Ducking his head and lowering his shoulders started a smooth descent, while craning his neck up and lifting his arms sent him skyward again. He dipped and rose and raced above the yard.

Nick descended and streaked toward Gorilla-Burger. The great ape spread his arms out, ready to corral the flying robot. But Nick shot up and over him at the last second, just escaping the grasping hands. Gorilla-Burger roared.

Nick zoomed another circle around the yard. On his way back to the beast, he swooped down and picked up the discarded bucket. Then he flew straight over Gorilla-Burger and jammed the upside-down bucket over his head on the way past.

The great ape ran blindly after him, using both hands to try to get the bucket unstuck. Nick turned his head and watched over his shoulder. The image brought the abstract concept of humor to the forefront of his thought process, although he didn't know exactly why that—

Clang!

His metal boots clipped the top of the playhouse. Grass and sky changed places again and again as he flipped through the air. The elm tree rushed up to smash him. He pulled his shoulders aside and just missed it as he flew by. But he was still spinning out of control. How was he supposed to steer when he couldn't even tell where up ended and down started to—

Smash!

A section of gutter shook loose as Nick collided with the house. The rocket boosters were still engaged and scraped him along the side.

Nick pushed off with his arms, separating from the house. But something felt very wrong. The rockets were stuck on high speed. He zoomed over the yard, much too fast. He was headed straight for the tree. There wouldn't be enough time to swerve around the—

Crash!

Nick barreled right through a thick cluster of tree limbs. Splintered branches rained down onto the lawn.

The rockets cut out. Nick, eye portals closed and metal arms covering his head, dropped down to thud on the grass. He lay there, cringing, expecting the worst. But there was no pain.

The unexpected catastrophe had woken the Nick part of him. He was suddenly worried about the damage he'd done to Burger's house, his mom having to take him to the hospital again, that strange delivery truck at the bottom of the hill. Everything.

Gorilla-Burger popped into sight, hovering over him. He frantically gibbered out monkey sounds, eyes wide as hubcaps. His movements were herky-jerky, not the smooth animal reflexes of a few moments before. He looked more like Burger. Maybe the crash had snapped him back into his own senses as much as it had Nick.

Now that he was on the ground, Jax had regained his courage, and he pranced around both of them, helpfully barking his head off.

Gorilla-Burger lowered his hands to the fallen robot, gingerly checking his arms and his chest plate.

"I'M FINE, BURGER," Nick recited in his mechanical voice. "NOW GET YOUR HAIRY MITTS OFF ME. WE REALLY NEED TO—"

Nick raised his head up off the grass.

His audio sensors picked up the distant slamming of a car door.

Then words: "I need to grab the groceries out of the back. You girls go ahead inside." The sound was faint, but very clear.

Oh, no.

"BURGER. IT'S YOUR MOM. SHE'S HOME."

8

GORILLA-BURGER'S EYES GREW EVEN WIDER SOME-
how. He gripped himself under the ears with both hands
and grunted with effort. Nick realized he was trying to
pull the mask off. But all he managed to do was yank out
tufts of matted hair and growl in pain.

"YOU HAVE TO PULL THE ZIPPER FIRST, IT'S ALL CON-
NECTED," Nick intoned. "HURRY."

The hairy beast lifted his head to the sky and clawed
at his throat. Nick was struck by a strong bout of déjà vu
—where had he seen that before?—but he was more concerned that those gorilla fingers looked way too thick to
grab the tiny end of the zipper.

"COME HERE, LET ME TRY TO—"

Nick's audio sensors picked up the opening of the front door, and then the thumping of little feet racing down the main hall. He knew that hallway led right to the sliding-glass door in back, and pretty soon—

"Eeeeeeee!"

"Aaaaaaah!"

Burger's five-year-old twin sisters stood on the back porch in matching pink overalls, wailing like B-movie scream queens. Then they disappeared back into the house.

"Girls! What's going on?"

Nick heard Burger's mom hurry down the hallway.

"Mom! There's a gorilla in the backyard!"

"And a robot!"

"*What?*"

Nick clamped a metallic hand on Gorilla-Burger's elbow and they raced to the playhouse. The ape kicked the door open and ducked, trying to squeeze through headfirst, but everything about the twins' playhouse was half size. His fuzzy butt and hind legs stuck out as black fur filled every inch of the door frame.

Burger's mom's rushed footsteps were nearly at the back door. Nick commanded his rocket boosters to turn on for just half a second, and he launched himself at Gorilla-Burger's backside.

Smash! They both popped through the door together, a tangled mass of metal and fur. Somehow, Nick managed to reach behind and shut the door. There was hardly any room to breathe, much less to move.

"Michael? Michael, honey, are you back here? Are you …Oh my goodness, what happened?" A fresh round of screams from Burger's little sisters punctuated his mom's question. "What have you done this time?"

"WE NEED TO GET THESE COSTUMES OFF. QUICK." Nick tried to whisper, but apparently the mechanical voice only had one volume setting.

"Is that you in there? Why do you sound so odd?" The door shook in its frame, but Gorilla-Burger blocked it with the splayed toes of a massive foot. "Michael Edward Hindberg, you get out of your sisters' playhouse this instant."

Nick raked his metal fingers through the fur at the base of Gorilla-Burger's neck, over and over. Finally an option occurred to him:

MAGNETIZE DIGITS?

Yes.

Nick's fingers, buried deep in fur, met the zipper clasp with a *clink*. He pulled down.

The fur fell away and Burger flopped out, steaming with sweat. There was suddenly much more room to maneuver in the playhouse. Burger looked down at the costume, bundled up around his ankles. "That was so awesome!" he whispered fiercely.

Nick jerked his thumb at the door.

Burger nodded. "It's okay, Mom," he called. "It's just me and Nick."

"Whatever are you doing in there? Your sisters said they saw something very strange."

"It's nothing. We just picked up some Halloween costumes and were messing around with them."

Nick lifted his arm and motioned to his side. Burger undid a few clasps and the costume fell from around Nick's body. He could suddenly *feel* again—the chilled moisture in the air, the sweaty hair plastered to his head. He seemed so exposed that he almost felt naked.

"You weren't playing that horrible Movie Fight game again, were you?"

"No way, Mom."

She scoffed. "Sure. Well, you two come on inside and get something to eat, anyway. But first clean up this mess and stop scaring your sisters."

They could both hear her walking away. When Nick exhaled, it felt like the first time he had done so in hours.

Both of the boys stared at the limp forms of the gorilla and the robot, then looked up at each other.

"I don't think these are normal costumes," Burger said.

"Good observation, detective."

"No. I mean, there's more. I didn't think I was... I mean, I didn't know that..." Burger's face went purple in his struggle to articulate.

"What?"

Burger shook his head. "I didn't feel like myself."

Nick could relate. "You know something else about these costumes?" He held up the gorilla.

"What?"

"I don't think that was a real grizzly bear at the bottom of the cliff."

PART II

THE
DELIVERYMAN

A forest outside Salem, Massachusetts
The previous night

CONNOR FLANAGAN CLUTCHED A SCRAP OF hospital stationery in a sweaty fist, his other hand struggling with the oversize steering wheel of his dad's delivery truck. The gangly redhead tried to make out words in the dark, but the handwriting was almost as shaky as his grip. His father had scrawled out the directions mere moments before choking out a final breath.

But there had been no time for Connor to mourn the sudden passing of Connor Sr. "Go," the older man had wheezed, dropping the paper in Connor's lap. "Tonight."

The delivery truck jounced over rocks and crunched

through half-frozen puddles. Just a few miles back, he had been on a well-maintained country road. But when Connor squeezed the truck through that hidden left turn into the forest, trees had closed in on both sides of the deeply rutted single-lane path. Bare branches scraped along the side panels with a screeching that sounded almost human.

The bizarre bits of advice from his father, delivered in a strangled whisper, floated through Connor's frazzled brain.

Avoid eye contact.

Don't ask too many questions.

Remember everything you're told.

He swallowed heavily and tried to focus on the last thing his dad had said while grabbing Connor's wrist with surprising strength.

Don't be afraid, son. They shouldn't hurt you.

A hawk screamed nearby. Without thinking, Connor used the scrap of paper to mop his clammy forehead. When he realized what he was doing, he jerked the paper away to find the ink all smeared. "Oh, good gravy," he muttered, the closest he ever came to swearing.

But it didn't matter. The last few lines were still legible:

Dead end at ridge.
Turn right.
Straight through the holly.

When Connor looked back up, he nearly smashed into an outcropping of rock over ten feet high. The truck lurched to a stop. He stared through the passenger-side window and could just make out, through the swirling snowflakes and the darkness, a wall of holly bushes.

Connor glanced at the clock on the dashboard and let out his breath in a shuddering sigh. Was there a worse time than midnight to be blundering your way to some mysterious destination in the middle of the wilderness?

They shouldn't hurt you.

He whispered it aloud a few times, trying to convince himself. But *shouldn't* was not the same thing as *wouldn't*.

Finally, Connor gripped the wheel in both hands and wrenched it to the right. He inhaled deeply, pressed on the gas pedal, and muscled the truck right through the thorny bushes.

He emerged into a small clearing, tires flattening the pile of dead leaves. A dilapidated collection of boards and logs—more abandoned shack than country cottage— huddled against the base of a hill.

Connor brought the truck to a stop a few yards from the front door. The grimy windows revealed nothing but blackness within, and no smoke rose from the crumbling chimney.

Should he get out? Connor couldn't remember his father saying what to do if the place was empty. With a sharp pang of grief that lanced straight through his chest, Connor realized that his dad would never tell him anything again.

And even though it shamed him, the sorrow was followed by a sigh of relief. Maybe he wouldn't have to go in, after all; maybe he could just turn around and forget all about—

The door opened. Or had it simply fallen off its tired hinges and collapsed inward?

Connor pushed open his own door and stepped down from the delivery truck, pulling the collar of his jacket up around his ears. His insides fluttered wildly, making it hard to draw a normal breath, as he stretched his long legs over a few fallen slats of wood. Probably the ghost of a long-dead fence.

He still couldn't believe he was here, wherever (and whatever) *here* was. Connor gulped, his knobby Adam's apple bobbing up and down, and ducked his head to peer into the doorway. "Hello?"

A young woman stepped out of the shack holding an oil lantern. Aside from the old-fashioned clothing —homespun dress and plain white bonnet—she could have been one of his classmates at the dental college. And she was even pretty. Blond hair spilled out from under her head covering and framed a heart-shaped face.

Connor gulped. This was so not what he was expecting that he had no idea what he should say. What was she doing out here? It certainly didn't seem very safe. And what could she possibly have to do with his dad?

The young woman lifted the lantern and studied Connor's face while he stood there, shivering and speechless. She smiled at him and inclined her head daintily toward his dad's truck. Finally, she spoke.

"Pizza delivery?"

Connor gasped and choked on his own spittle. After a coughing jag, he spluttered out, *"What?"*

"It's about time, good sir. You didn't make it here in under thirty minutes, so I get it free, right?"

Connor stared. "But...I don't...why would you—"

She put her hand over her mouth and giggled. "Oh, I do apologize. But you should have seen your face." More laughing, and it went on so long that she had to wipe her eyes. "Absolutely priceless!"

He stood up straighter, tried to gather himself. Eventually, she stopped laughing.

"Oh, all right, I'll stick to the script. I always forget how serious you city folk are the first time you come out here." She cleared her throat. "'Who is it that comes here this night?'" Her voice sounded deeper, more official.

Connor tried to remember the exact phrasing from his father. The formal words felt awkward in his mouth. "'I...uh...I am the next. The line remains unbroken.'"

"Well, we'll see about that, won't we? Step closer, please. There we go. And hold this for me, if you would." She handed him the oil lantern.

The woman then grasped his free hand in her own. Her flesh was soft, but the grip hinted at bones of steel underneath.

Her other hand reached into a pocket in the folds of her dress, and reappeared holding a hunting knife longer than her forearm.

"Aaaah!" Connor instinctively recoiled. He tried to pull free and dash back to the truck. But that iron grip held steady and he ended up looking like those cartoon characters that rev up by running in place.

"Ooooooh, my, my! Aren't you a skittish thing?" She giggled again, but the sound had a raspier quality now. Connor squirmed like a fish on a line. "Hold still, it's just a little test. Need to make sure you're the father's son." She pulled his hand closer, the knife darted out with a *snick*, and Connor's thumb started bleeding from an inch-long gash.

He was shocked into stillness, staring at the red line dripping down into his palm. Had she just mentioned a test? What, like a DNA blood test? This place didn't exactly look like it was equipped with the kind of medical equipment it would take to—

The woman thrust her head forward and jammed Connor's thumb into her mouth. He shuddered in revulsion but remained frozen to the spot.

She closed her eyes and made greedy slurping sounds. Connor experienced a brand-new emotion: too scared to throw up.

Just as he began to feel light-headed from blood loss, she pulled his thumb out of her mouth with a little *pop!*

The woman titled her face thoughtfully to the side, smacking her lips gingerly, as if testing out free samples at a Ben & Jerry's counter. "Irish mixed with a dash of Norwegian. Blue-collar roots. A little low in iron, but a robust flavor all the same." She licked the few remaining drops of blood from the tip of his thumb. "Yes, I'd say you're definitely his son, all right."

She finally released Connor's wrist and he stumbled backward. Then he jammed his hand into the front pocket of his jeans, not able to even look at his thumb anymore.

The woman took back her lantern and pointed at the delivery truck behind him, then tilted her head to indicate the knoll beside the house. "If you would be so kind as to back your carriage up to the side of the hill there, between those bushes. Open up the doors nice and wide. I have your first delivery job all ready to go."

Connor cleared his throat. "Oh, um, actually, I wanted to talk to you about that."

Her eyes narrowed. "Yes...?"

"Well, you see, the thing is that I have midterms starting on Monday." She just stared at him. "So I have, you know, a lot of studying to do." More staring. "So I thought that, maybe, we could..."

She crossed her arms over her chest. The stare was definitely more of a glare now. "Do go on."

"...thought maybe we could, if possible, postpone the delivery?" He took a deep breath and rushed on. "Just by a week or so, until I'm able to—"

"You thought *what???*" the woman snarled.

And then the right side of her face melted.

Or at least that's what it looked like to Connor's horrified eyes. The skin around her mouth went slack and drooped down right past her chin. Her cheeks got all doughy and seemed to slide down into her neck. And the flesh on her forehead suddenly appeared ancient— wrinkles on top of wrinkles—and oozed down until it covered her right eye.

"Oh, dear me," the woman said. She scooped up all of that sagging skin in two hands and pressed it against her face. Then she chanted a rapid stream of words that Connor didn't understand, but it sounded like one of those guttural languages where the words have eight consonants in a row. Maybe German? And when she took her hands away, her face looked as young and pretty as before.

"My apologies. That happens when I get...*upset*... sometimes."

She fixed Connor with a pointed stare. "You don't want to make me upset, do you?"

"No, ma'am." It was the truth.

"Oooooh, 'no, *ma'am*,' is it? My, my, my. You're just as polite as your great-great-grandfather was. Look a bit like him, too." She reached up with one little hand and felt a lock of Connor's red hair between her fingers. It took all of his willpower to stand still and not scream. He definitely did not want to make her upset again. "Yep, same complexion as old Jedidiah Flanagan. You two could've been twins." She winked at him. "Although I'm not exactly saying that as a compliment." She cackled out more of that raspy laughter and then burped, a small blood bubble forming and bursting at the edge of her mouth. She dabbed at it daintily with the sleeve of her robe.

Don't be afraid, son.

Connor focused on the words, realizing his dad must have been in this exact same position. Even though he felt nauseated with terror, Connor couldn't go back on a deathbed promise to his father.

And he desperately wanted to ask how she could possibly have known his great-great-grandfather, but he also remembered his dad's instructions about questions.

"Now, are you going to bring that delivery truck over here so that we can get started?"

Connor turned and hurried back to the truck, fighting to keep dinner in his stomach. He revved the engine and briefly considered stomping on the gas to plow right back through the holly bushes. Instead—with the image of his father's face fixed in his mind—he backed the truck up to the little hill and swung open the back panels.

When he stepped back out of the truck, he saw the woman waving her hands in front of the little knoll, chanting out more of those harsh-sounding words. Then a bright line appeared right down the middle of the hill, dividing it in half. It reminded him of the sliver of light under a bedroom door.

The entire hill shook, ground trembling like an earthquake, and the whole thing split apart. Gradually a torchlit cavern was revealed through a rough rectangle about twenty feet wide, the edges of the opening marked by ripped-up roots and worms squirming in the freshly exposed soil.

The woman disappeared into the shack. Connor heard scraping noises coming from inside the cavern and stepped away.

Then he saw someone—or was it some*thing?*—loading up the truck. He could only make out a shadowy figure, but something about the hulking shape and lurching movements hinted at a being not entirely human. It was too bulky, the outline of the body choppy instead of smooth. It looked like a figure patched together out of broken cinder blocks.

But that was crazy. Right? Connor breathed deeply, trying to maintain his grip on reality. He shifted his eyes from the cavern and settled on the truck, comforting because it was such a familiar sight from his childhood. That truck had sat in his parents' driveway for over twenty years. Connor had seen it every day of his life before he left for dental school just a few months ago.

The lumbering *thing* loading the truck made a low moaning noise. Connor glanced at the cavern to make sure it wasn't coming out to eat him or anything. The thing moved its arm clumsily back and forth. What was it—could it be trying to wave?

Light from the torch spilled onto the form, and it looked slathered in mud. Thick slabs of wet earth covered its entire frame, the stubby ends of twigs sprouting out all over. Almost as if... could that thing actually be made entirely of mud?

Connor refocused his gaze on the truck, forced himself to concentrate on it. Dad had always told him that he used the rig for his job, delivering furniture all over Massachusetts for a company based in Wakefield.

But Connor was starting to seriously doubt that was the case.

How could his life have gone so far off the rails, so quickly? Two days ago he had been in a nice, safe classroom, listening to a lecture on impacted molars. Now he was here, freezing and gripped by terror, grinding his own molars into enamel dust.

The woman shuffled out the front door, made her way over to him, and shoved a rolled-up piece of paper into his hands.

Connor unfurled the paper to find a crudely drawn map of America. Only instead of being divided up into states, there were a series of winking, multicolored lights covering the landmass.

He flipped the paper over—it had to be hooked up to a battery or something to be powering those lights—but there was nothing on the other side except some oil stains.

The woman reached up and pointed to a spot on the map. "Delivery needs to be here. You've got a little less than forty-eight hours." She must have read Connor's facial expression, because she added, "Should be plenty of time. Your granddad could've made that delivery tonight and been back for breakfast." She tilted her head, apparently lost in memory. "He was the best. By far."

Connor gaped at the map. She was pointing to a spot in Washington State, clear on the other side of the country. He did the calculations in his head. "But that would..." He knew he was breaking several of his father's rules, but the words came rushing out. "...I mean, even if I drove a hundred miles per hour, day and night, with no stops, I'd never be able—"

The woman brushed aside his concerns with a wave of her hand. "Use the map. Your father told you about the map, didn't he? During your apprentice stage?"

Connor gulped. Had his dad been planning something like that—an apprenticeship to whatever was going on here? Before the stroke that hit without warning?

The memories burst through a dam he hadn't even known he'd built in his mind and they flooded his thoughts. All of his dad's invitations to come along for the ride on deliveries—especially after Connor got his driver's license—Connor had always declined. Too busy. And his dad said the same thing every time: "Don't blame ya. Everyone has to grow up and face some pretty tough stuff. But that day is not today, my boy. Enjoy yourself."

It was too late for any of that now.

He shook his head at the creepy woman.

She blew out her breath in exasperation, the skin around her mouth going all droopy again and sloughing off her face. She quickly shoved it back into place. "Okay, listen close." She pointed at the lights and explained how to use the map along with a couple of most unusual accessories in the truck.

But he still didn't believe any of it. Not really. Not yet.

"Use the map and you won't go wrong. Can't have you out on the streets too much with our special cargo, can we?" She rolled up the map and thrust it back at Connor.

The hulking, muddy man-shape finished loading up and slammed the back panels shut. Then it shuffled back into the cavern, and the hillsides rumbled together again. Connor wondered what else might be hidden underneath that mound of earth.

The woman gripped the edges of her dress with both hands, delicately between thumb and index finger, and did a formal little curtsy. It was such a contradiction to the sagging flesh and bloodsucking that it came across as grotesque. "Name used to be Mary. Mary Goodwin. Not anymore, but that's a good enough handle for city folk."

He nodded dumbly. "I'm Connor."

The creature formerly known as Mary Goodwin tsk-tsked. "Your family gets real creative with the names, don't they? You're the fourth Connor I've dealt with." She shook her head. "Now, I'm sure your daddy at least gave a warning about what would happen—to you—if anything goes wrong with these little beauties in here." She tapped on a side panel with a crooked finger to indicate the cargo within. Connor realized that he hadn't even thought about *what* he would be delivering, and he suddenly got more nervous about climbing into the truck than he was about staying here with her.

"What, um, exactly is it that I'll be...?"

She glared at him again, and he remembered his dad's warning about too many questions. "Never you mind. It's different every time." She patted the side of the truck. "Tomorrow's Halloween, so this is a bit of a specialty order. But you're just the deliveryman, understand? You'll be compensated after a successful run. I've always taken care of your family. *Always*." She leaned in closer, the skin trembling as if threatening to droop right off her face again, and her breath smelled like wood smoke and dirt. "And never forget our number one rule: destruction before detection. The outside world must never learn what we're doing here. Understood?"

Connor nodded slowly.

But he didn't understand anything.

9

NICK DUMPED HIS BIKE IN THE GRAVEL DRIVEWAY
by his mom's Dodge hatchback. If he and Burger were
seriously going to risk their lives by hiking back to grizzly-
infested woods and investigating an abandoned delivery
truck full of costumes with special powers ... well, then,
he was going to need two pieces of cinnamon toast and
some chocolate milk.

He eased the front door open quietly—his mom had
been keeping pretty weird hours over the last few months
and he never knew when she would be sleeping.

He found a note on the kitchen counter:

Hey sweets,

I worked a double last night at the mill, so I'm taking a nap before the Hungry Lumberjack dinner rush. There's a box of casserole helper and a can of tuna in the cupboard. Just use water instead of milk. (I'll get groceries this weekend and that's a promise!!) If you hang out with Burger, do it at his house, okay? Unless he learned how to be quiet—ha ha!

P.S. On Sunday I have a real day off—no mill or restaurant shifts at all. Yay! And Crazy Mike's is having a 99-cent movie rental special this week. Let's get some spooky movies and scare ourselves silly on the day after Halloween! I'll even pick up some of that horrible cheese-flavored popcorn you like if you agree to hang out with your mom for the afternoon.

Love,
Mom

At the bottom of the note was a doodle that looked like a fat dog but that Nick knew was supposed to be the teddy bear he had when he was little. It was the only thing his mom could halfway draw, and she put it at the bottom of all her notes to him.

He set his backpack on the counter and tiptoed over to the fridge. He reached up to the top of it and pulled down the metal coffee can with the word *Tips* scrawled across the side in black marker. It was the money his mom used for groceries. And utilities. And gas for the hatchback. And entertainment. Everything except the rent, basically.

And—okay, who was he kidding?—probably even to help cover rent, sometimes, if the child support check didn't show up.

He popped off the lid and looked inside. Must have been a slow week at the Lumberjack—just a few wrinkled bills at the bottom. Mostly singles. Definitely not enough for groceries.

Or maybe things hadn't been slow. Nick hadn't seen his dad in over two years, and he had a suspicion that the child support check hadn't shown up since then, either. But his mom had never complained, at least not to Nick.

He snuck a peek at her bedroom door. He sure didn't want his mom to catch him in the act of doing this, especially after reading that note.

Nick set the coffee can on the counter. When he was sure that he hadn't woken her up, he reached into his pocket, grabbed the money he had made at school that day, and dropped the bills into the can. It had been a good day—maybe there would even be enough for his mom to buy the garden stuff she wanted.

It was their unspoken arrangement. Nick pretended like he wasn't a major contributor to their household income, and his mom never asked where all the extra money in the tips can was coming from.

There was never enough left over to start a bank account. College would have to be paid for with scholarships, or not at all.

Burger asked about the money almost every day—why didn't Nick buy cool games like Zombie Golf, or a phone, or at least get himself a decent bike?

But Nick couldn't tell Burger. He wouldn't understand; he had a dad, a good one.

Or maybe Burger *would* understand, but it was just too embarrassing. Whatever.

Before he returned the can, Nick remembered that his student account at the cafeteria was almost wiped out, so he grabbed a twenty and a ten and stuck them in his backpack. That would be enough for another month. Then he put the can back on top of the fridge and pushed it toward the back.

After he ate, Nick dropped the backpack on the couch, eased the front door open again, and grabbed his bike.

When Nick made his way around to the backyard again, Burger was reclining in a lounger and sipping a Coke while the robot cleaned up the mess from the Movie Fight.

Nick stopped and stared. "What did you . . . I mean, how is that—"

"This is so cool! Watch." Burger sat up in his chair. "Hey, robot! Pick up some more of those branches." The droid marched over to the scattered tree limbs that Nick had knocked loose while he was flying around with the rocket boosters. It bent stiffly at the waist, scooped up an armload of branches, and stood back up. Then it remained there, staring blankly into the middle distance. "Good work, robot. Now go dump them by the compost heap." The machine clanked over to the bin at the side of the house and dropped the branches.

Nick watched, horrified. "Burger," he breathed, "please tell me that you didn't trick your mom into trying on the costume."

Burger just laughed. "Of course not. What kind of guy do you take me for?"

Nick thought for a moment and then shook his head. "One of your sisters, then? That's almost as bad."

"Dude. I didn't put the costume on someone."

Nick pointed to the droid as it stood and stared at the compost heap. "Then how do you explain—"

"I put the costume on some*thing*."

Nick wrinkled up his eyebrows. "What, exactly, did you put the costume on?"

Burger leaned back and sipped his Coke again. "The lawn mower."

"The lawn mower?!"

Burger nodded.

"Why?"

"It was sitting by the garage, and I knew if my mom

noticed it, she'd make me mow the lawn before we took off." Burger shrugged. "So I threw the costume over it to hide the thing, and it just stood up and came at me."

"That's freaky."

"Totally. At first I thought it wanted to fight some more. But it turns out I could tell it what to do. Watch this." He turned to the droid and yelled, "Hey, robot! Do whatever you feel like."

The droid fell to all fours and started crawling around the backyard, pausing every few moments to take a huge bite of grass. Burger cracked up. "I guess old habits die hard."

Nick shook his head again. It was all just too weird. He had to admit, though, that Burger's act-first/think-later approach had yielded some interesting results. Although sometimes it was act-first/think-*never* that got them into trouble.

He watched the robot crawl around, chewing up the tall grass. That gave him an idea: Nick's mom was always joking about hiring a housekeeper—maybe their reward would be getting to keep one costume, and Nick could surprise her by putting the costume on a vacuum cleaner and turning it into a robo-maid. She'd love that. After she got over the freaking-out part.

And maybe he could take it to Hayley's Halloween party, too. He needed some way to catch her attention when they showed up, and he bet none of her rich friends had a robot butler.

But first they had work to do.

"Come on, Burger. Take that costume off the lawn mower and stash it in the garage—safely back in its box, please. Then we need to go find out if it's some*one* or some*thing* in that bear costume."

Somewhere in New Hampshire
Early the previous morning

CONNOR FLANAGAN REVVED THE DELIVERY
truck's engine, working up his nerve.

Ahead, the ring of purple light arced over the road like the entrance to some amusement park. A few minutes ago, he had hopped out of the truck and tried to approach on foot, examine it up close. But the light had disappeared, and he quickly learned that he could only see it through the windshield.

So it was true, what that creepy woman in the forest had said. The truck was special. Somehow equipped to deal with all of this craziness. The only vehicle on the planet that could navigate these things.

Connor gulped. Because if even half of what Mary Goodwin had said turned out to be true, he was in for one very interesting weekend.

He looked back down at the map spread out over the steering wheel. He had driven for more than two hours, crossing the border into New Hampshire to end up here, an old service road behind a railway station. The purple dot that glowed at this spot on the map was the closest circle of light to Salem, where his truck had been loaded up. And now the corresponding ring of light was facing him on the road, life-size and apparently real, blazing against the night sky.

As he stared at the light, Connor's memories took him back to the hospital room earlier that evening. Connor Sr. had started to babble, right at the end: *Wormholes... the map...tunnels through space and time...not impossible ...don't be afraid...*

There was more, but it was drowned out by the beeping of life-support machines as his body started to fail. When the doctors and nurses rushed in, they paid no attention to what they must have concluded were the incoherent ramblings of a fading mind. Connor had to admit he thought the same thing himself. Why would a mild-mannered furniture deliveryman be talking about wormholes?

He looked through the windshield again; apparently he was about to find out.

Frowning, he took one last look at the map. If he was reading it right, the corresponding light glowed across the country, near his delivery destination in Washington State.

But now he wasn't certain. Maybe that other light was more pinkish? How was he supposed to know for sure? He let his breath out in a frustrated snort. Even though Connor Sr. was often gone for days at a time, delivering "furniture" across New England, Connor had never missed his dad more—or been more mad at him, if he was being honest with himself—than at that moment.

The ring of light started to fade, shimmering until it was almost see-through in some parts. The surrounding night grew darker. He glanced nervously down at the map to find the purple dot was fading there, too. All over the map, these little colored lights were winking in and out of existence. He realized now that they never popped up in the same place. Who knew when—or where—he'd find the next close one?

"Oh, sure, wormhole travel can be a messy business," Mary Goodwin had told him in the forest. "But it sure beats standing in line at the airport with all of the other city fools." This was followed by cackling laughter on her part and uneasy silence from Connor.

He studied the map. Most of the wormhole lights

weren't near any roads; he was more likely to find one on top of a mountain or the bottom of a lake, if he was reading the map right. This could be his last chance to get the truck to the place where it was supposed to be and make the delivery on time. He did *not* want to think about what might happen to him if he failed.

Connor dropped his foot on the gas pedal and the truck lurched forward. The circle of light contracted. Just a moment earlier it had been big enough to drive an eighteen-wheel semi through. Now it was half that size.

The truck picked up speed, racing toward the diminishing circle. Connor's breath came in ragged gasps.

A family of raccoons scurried across the road and he swerved to miss them, then wrenched the steering wheel back to avoid plunging into a ditch. It felt like the truck nearly fell over on its side. Connor sighed in relief when it stayed upright, but as he rushed onward, he had a terrible thought: what if going through a wormhole *hurt*?

His body reacted automatically, foot slamming on the brake.

But it was too late; the front end squeezed through the opening before the brakes could fully engage.

Blazing sunshine filled the truck. Connor squeezed his eyes shut and threw his hands up in reflex. The seat belt tightened painfully across his chest as the truck slammed to a halt.

Connor eased his eyes open as they adjusted to the

intense new light. Through the dirty windshield he saw palm trees. A sandy beach. Waves crashing against the shore.

Opening his door felt like stepping into a steam bath. The shoreline continued ahead for a quarter mile or so before disappearing behind a rocky incline. Nothing beyond that but miles of open water. Was he on an island?

He turned around to check the coastline behind him and gasped. The truck was only half there. The front two wheels and the cab were stuck in the sand, but where the rear wheels and cargo bay should have been... just empty space. He waved his hand right through the area where the side panels should be.

He *was* on an island, he could see that now. And maybe not a very big one. The shoreline ended in a little green lagoon just ahead, and past that he could see the edge of the island curve back in on itself.

Breath coming in shallow gasps, he stuck his head through the door and looked to the rear. The back end of the truck was still there, filled with boxes of mysterious cargo. What the...?

Connor climbed into the cab and stepped behind the seats. He wedged his way down the narrow aisle in the rear of the truck, trying not to brush up against anything that might be stored there.

Connor put his shoulder against the back door and grunted with effort. Finally, it swung open.

The sky was dark on the service road. The light snow had turned to sleet, and a breeze splattered a few icy drops across his cheeks. His body shuddered violently, not accustomed to a fifty-degree drop in temperature from one end of a vehicle to the other.

He stepped down onto the asphalt, glancing at the rows of empty boxcars near the station across the street. Thankfully this was an isolated area; it would have been hard to explain his half-a-truck. Because here in New Hampshire the entire rig was sliced just as neatly in half, the rear end sitting in the middle of the road while the front set of wheels and cab were nowhere in sight.

Connor just stared. The night's whirlwind of emotions —from the heartbreak of the hospital room to the terror of Mary Goodwin's shack and, now, to *this*—caught up with him and he slumped against the side of the truck, his legs shaky.

Zzzzzt!

Connor smelled something acrid. He looked up and saw that the circle of purple light had constricted even further; the top edge was pressed right against the roof of the truck now. It sizzled and smoked where it touched, and seemed like it might be searing right through the metal.

Connor staggered back. The sides of the circle were closing in, touching the truck. He suddenly got a horrible flash of what could happen in the next few moments: the wormhole would slam shut completely, and he'd be left

here with half-a-truck full of who-knew-what and no way to move it. The service road was deserted now, but by morning somebody would come by. Maybe a police car.

He had been so freaked out by that woman and her melting face and her bloodsucking and her crazy instructions that he hadn't even bothered to think about whether all of this could be illegal. Could you be arrested for Participating in Extreme Weirdness?

Connor jumped into the truck's cargo area and rushed to the front seat, wincing again from the bright light. The view through the windshield was still a postcard from a tropical vacation.

He fired up the engine, threw the gearshift into reverse, and stomped on the gas pedal. The wheels spun, spraying sand everywhere, but the truck didn't budge. He mashed the pedal to the floor, the engine screaming in protest, but still no movement.

Connor hopped out. The purple light circle was mere inches away from the side of the truck and closing fast. Black smoke drifted into the sky from where the roof was already being eaten away by purple flame.

He had to do something. Now. What if this was a deserted island? He'd rather take his chances with the New Hampshire State Patrol. He didn't think he'd be able to sail back to civilization in the cab of a truck.

The spinning wheels had dug trenches in the sand. Connor leaned in and grabbed his jacket off the passenger seat, then wedged it under a front tire for traction.

The same thing sometimes worked in snow and ice back home.

He hopped back into the truck and punched the gas. The front wheels spun for a second, but then caught on the material, getting a little purchase and sending the truck reeling backward.

The world went dark again. The tires left a patch of burning rubber on the asphalt as Connor rocketed in reverse down the deserted service road.

Finally, his head cleared and he stomped on the brakes. The ring of purple light collapsed in on itself, becoming a tiny dot of purple in midair before winking out of existence.

Connor slumped against the steering wheel, exhausted, and slipped into self-pity mode. Who else could have possibly ever had a night as messed up as this one?

Then it came to him. His dad, that's who.

Connor Sr. must have gone through something like this before. Heck, he certainly must have seen worse, if he had been making these special deliveries for years and years. Providing for Connor and his mom. And he never heard his dad complain about his job. Not once.

That gave him some resolve. Connor picked his head back up, grabbed the map, and started looking for the next available wormhole.

10

THE BOYS WERE RUNNING DOWN THE HIDDEN trail, half exhilarated and half terrified at the prospect of returning to that truck full of incredible costumes, when Burger grabbed Nick by the shoulders and shoved him behind a tree.

"Hey, what are you—"

Burger clamped his hand over Nick's mouth and dropped to the ground, pulling his friend down with him. Nick's chest slammed into the forest floor, then Burger's bulk was pressing against his back, making it impossible to breathe. The costume that Burger had been carrying spilled into the mud, clumps of pine needles clinging to the gorilla fur.

Burger put one finger over his lips, then slowly let go of Nick and pointed around the tree and through a clump of bushes.

Nick held his breath and peered out, expecting to see the bear.

But it was Chet Millard and his friends. Which was even worse. At least grizzlies attacked out of necessity. High schoolers did it for sport.

Chet was in his off-road wheelchair. Instead of tires, it had treads like you'd see on a military tank, plus overhead roll bars like a dune buggy. A machete was strapped to the back for hacking through underbrush.

He had nine friends with him. Two pairs of guys were hauling silver kegs down the hill, three more were making a circle of rocks in the center of a clearing, and a couple more were picking up fallen branches and stacking them up inside the circle, preparing for a bonfire.

One guy grabbed a steel cable attached to a winch on the back of Chet's chair and hooked it around the base of a birch tree. Chet revved up his machine, thrusting his armrest controls at full throttle as the tank treads gripped the forest floor, and finally the tree was ripped from the ground, roots and all. Chet dragged it over to the bonfire pit, waving and smiling as his friends cheered. Then he drew that machete and circled the tree, hacking off the branches.

"Setting up for one of their stupid parties," Nick

whispered. Burger nodded grimly. Both boys remembered the last time one of Chet's parties had veered too close to their domain.

Last spring the boys had spent over two months building the coolest fort in the history of adolescent architecture. It had a real door with hinges, scavenged from the dump. A rope ladder led to a second-story tower, where you could launch a slingshot or escape into the overhanging branches of a fir tree. There was even a watertight storage area to hold snacks and comics and stuff. Located close to a little cove on the bay with some good boulders for diving, the fort was going to be the perfect hangout for summer break.

Construction was completed on the last day of school. On the first morning of vacation, they had hiked down with armloads of supplies to get the place stocked. Best summer ever, straight ahead.

But the deluxe fort had been smashed to pieces. And then burned.

Nick and Burger didn't have any proof, but Chet and his friends were the only names on the suspect list.

"Can't let them see us," Burger breathed. Nick pushed himself backward, staying low, trying to put some distance between him and the screen of undergrowth before standing up and running away.

"Where you think you're going?" The voice came from right behind them. Nick and Burger turned to see a big slab of meat with a shaved head and letterman's jacket looming over them. "Hey, guys, look what I found," he called.

Shouting. Swearwords. Feet stomping on the sodden ground. Hands grabbing at Nick and jerking him into the air. It all blurred together until he was slammed against an oak tree.

Ox Kramme, offensive lineman for Bayside High, had his cement block of a hand wrapped around Nick's throat to pin him against the trunk.

The rest of the high schoolers swarmed all around. "The fat one ran off." Ox jerked his head over his shoulder, indicating the forest on the other side of the trail. "Go find him."

Three guys crashed through the ferns after Burger. The rest stood in a semicircle around Ox, sneering at Nick. He was even more scared than when the bear was chasing him.

And finally there was Chet, wheelchair treads churning up the mud and rolling smoothly over the exposed tree roots in the path. He regarded Nick with a casual smile as if they had all met up in the lobby of the movie theater downtown.

"Well, hello. What were you lovebirds doing out here? Building another nest?"

So it was true: Chet and his friends had destroyed their dream fort. Nick clenched his jaw but didn't say anything.

Ox squeezed, his cold fingers digging into the side of Nick's neck. "Chet asked you a question."

"Nothing," he wheezed. *Can't. Let them know. About the truck full of costumes.* "Just walking around. Exploring."

Shouts from the guys looking for Burger drifted back from deeper in the woods. Sounded like questions. Apparently they hadn't found him yet. Good.

"Is that right?" Chet said. "Because it kind of looks like you were spying on us."

Nick tried to shake his head no, but he couldn't move within Ox's grip. The oversize teen squeezed again and his meaty palm pressed Nick's Adam's apple into his throat. Nick's vision went dark and fuzzy for a moment.

He was so scared that his whole body went numb. Some part of his brain knew Ox didn't actually want to kill him, but he couldn't trust him to know exactly when to stop squeezing, either. Isn't this how people died? Stupid accidents like this?

He opened his mouth to beg Ox to let him go, but only a strangled whisper came out.

"What was that? Didn't quite catch it." Chet's chair edged closer and he leaned forward, tilting his head toward Nick as if he were trying to listen. He was close enough that Nick could feel his breath against his face.

Nick had a sickening thought: if Chet punched him in the stomach right now, and knocked the wind out of him with Ox still gripping his throat, it really could kill him. What if he—

And that's when he noticed the gorilla costume.

It wasn't there anymore.

Chet's eyes narrowed. "What are you grinning about? I say something funny?"

I'm smiling because you're about to be visited by a gorilla on a rampage. And yes, I think it's hilarious, actually.

One of the searchers, a lean wide receiver with dark hair, stumbled back onto the trail. "We can't find him, Chet. Could be anywhere."

Probably swinging way up in the branches, Tarzan-style, ready to drop down right on your heads! Despite not being able to breathe much, Nick felt his smile get even bigger.

Chet wheeled around and yelled at the guy. "Come on, did you see the size of that kid? How hard can it be to find a fat boy with no camouflage running around in the woods?"

The dark-haired teen shrugged and looked at the ground. "It's a big forest."

Chet looked around at his surrounding group of friends. "Anybody got an idea how we can catch him?"

A guy with a single black eyebrow stretched low across his forehead, caveman-style, grinned and pointed at Nick. "Maybe if this one starts screaming, the other one will come running back for him."

Nick got even more nervous. But not for himself this time. The thought suddenly came to him: when Gorilla-Burger (finally) attacked, was he going to be able to control himself? Things had gotten overly heated in the backyard, and that was just a play fight between friends. What if the power of the costume put him into a serious rage?

A hideous scene flashed before Nick's eyes: blood splattered against the tree trunks as Gorilla-Burger ripped the high schoolers apart, unable to control himself.

As much as he wanted to stop these guys from hurting him and Burger, he didn't want anyone to die. He had to warn them, get Chet and all of his stupid friends to hustle up the trail and return to the SUV.

Ox was watching Chet and the redhead. Nick slapped at his forearm to get his attention. The thing was hard as a two-by-four.

Ox turned, annoyed. "What are you doing?"

Too late. Nick saw a flash of black fur through the screen of brush behind the guys. Things were about to get very ugly.

He grabbed at Ox's fingers, thick as bratwursts, and tried to pry them off of his throat.

"Oh, no you don't." Ox tightened his grip. Nick's vision went fuzzy again and he lost feeling in his legs.

At least I tried to warn them.

It was his last thought before Gorilla-Burger smashed through a thicket of bushes.

At least I tried.

10½

Northern Alaska
A couple of hours earlier

CONNOR BONKED HIS HEAD AGAINST THE STEER-
ing wheel in frustration. Then he lifted it and looked out
the windshield one more time. Then he bonked it against
the steering wheel again.

This couldn't be Washington State. Not with this much
snow in October. The surrounding trees were indistin-
guishable white lumps, while drifts piled up around the
truck, several feet high. Connor couldn't tell if he was
even on a road at all.

And then there was the moose herd. There must have
been at least fifty of them crowding around the truck,

snorting steam through enormous black nostrils. They didn't *look* particularly menacing, but Connor had a feeling those enormous antlers weren't designed for purely decorative purposes.

He checked the rearview mirror. The wormhole—this one a circle of blazing orange—stood out in stark contrast against the snow-blanketed background.

Being stuck here would be even worse than the deserted island. He wrenched the gearshift into reverse and punched the gas, but the truck was stuck in the snowdrift. He'd have to go out there and dig it out.

Time to bonk the ol' head against the steering wheel again.

Finally, Connor eased the door open and was hit by an icy blast of air. That's when he remembered that his jacket was still lying on a beach somewhere. He shut the door. Dying of frostbite was not going to help.

He peeked into the back of the truck, hoping for a scrap of tarp or maybe a burlap sack—any kind of protection from the arctic wind.

One of the boxes had tipped over. Was that a bit of a fur coat poking out? His luck couldn't be that good, not on this night. But Connor reached back and grabbed the box anyway, setting it on his lap.

He opened it. His frayed nerves finally broke and he let out a little scream. There was a life-size bear head glaring up at him, face frozen in midsnarl. What the...?

The sound of moose bumping into the truck outside

pulled Connor out of his shock. He grabbed the fur in two hands and lifted. The box fell to the floor and a bearskin rug unfurled across his lap and draped itself over the passenger seat.

Too weird.

He heard another thud and looked up to find a huge, hairy face pressed right up against the windshield, smearing moose snot all over the glass. Connor looked at those antlers and realized that a quarter inch of glass was all that kept him from a wild animal and subzero temperatures.

He looked back down at the bearskin. If he could drape this over himself, and all the moose got a look at that fearsome bear face...was there a chance they would back off and let him get back in the truck? And if that didn't work, at least he would die warm. The thing really was just basically a big fur coat.

There was barely enough room in the cab to allow him to stand up. Connor lifted the bearskin and noticed a zipper running down the chest. Was it some kind of costume?

He grabbed the zipper at the base of the bear's throat and yanked down. Several of the moose moved forward and tilted their heads to study him through the glass, and a few started snorting in earnest.

He hurried to get both legs inside and then worked his arms in there as well. It was warm, all right, although after he got all the way in he realized it was maybe *too* warm. It felt moist, almost, as if someone had been jogging in it recently, sweating and breathing hot air that had been trapped inside.

One of the moose lowered its head and shifted its weight to its haunches. Was it actually going to charge the truck?

Panicked, Connor grabbed the zipper in one of his paw-hands and pulled it all the way up to his chin.

And that's when things started to get *seriously* strange.

WHEN GORILLA-BURGER SMASHED THROUGH THE thicket of ferns, Nick braced himself, ready to leap into action as soon as Ox loosened his grip. He might have to thrust his body in between the charging beast and the group of high school guys so there was at least a chance that nobody got killed. With any luck they would all turn and run, screaming, when they saw that powerful beast up close. When they were confronted by a wild animal, face-to-face, without the protection of the bars of a zoo cage in between, the pure terror of the situation should be enough to—

Wait.

No one was running. Or screaming.

There was some laughing, though.

The wiry, black-haired guy looked around at his friends and jerked a thumb at Gorilla-Burger. "Is he serious?"

Nick turned his attention from the older teenagers to his friend. Gorilla-Burger was waving his paws in the air, snarling and shaking his head.

But the fur sagged and hung in loose folds. His oversize mask flopped around, cheeks sunken in on an expressionless face. Instead of a full-throated primal roar, the sound that came out was sort of a muffled snuffling. And he was about half the size he had been in the backyard.

Two guys sauntered up to Gorilla-Burger, grabbed him by the upper arms, spun him around, and slammed him against the tree next to Nick.

Burger turned to look at his friend, eyes peering out from inside a lifeless rubbery mask.

"Dude. I don't think the costumes are working anymore."

"Yeah, I noticed that," Nick wheezed out before Ox squeezed his throat even more tightly.

Nick was so terrified it would have been hard to breathe even without Ox's fingers wrapped around his neck. He had seen the way these guys smashed into each other on the football field. If that's what they did for fun, then what would they do to him and Burger? Plus, they would probably not be handing out helmets first.

Chet powered his chair right up to the boys. He grabbed the overhead roll bar with those powerful arms and pulled himself up so he was looking down at Burger.

He scanned the gorilla costume up and down. "So...I guess Smoke Valley kids must do Halloween early. What, do you need the extra candy to feed your families?"

Nick thought about the lonely tips can on top of the fridge and his face got hot.

Ox looked over at Chet. "Come on, man, can we just throw a beating on them and get it over with?"

"Yeah," another guy said. "If we're not on the field by six for warm-ups, Coach is not going to be happy."

And that's when Nick felt a little bit of hope. He realized these guys wanted something, and that Nick and Burger could actually provide it. Supply and demand. Simple.

Time for a negotiation.

But first he had to get free so that he could talk. While he wasn't proud of it, Nick could only think of one way. He worked up a bunch of saliva and let it spill out of his mouth and slobber down his chin.

Ox was looking at Chet when he felt the drool spread across his hand and wrist. "Oh, nasty!" He let go and stepped away, rubbing his hand on his jeans.

Nick moved fast. He stepped up to Chet and said, "You know, it's probably not a real good idea to beat us up."

"Is that right?" Chet made a big show out of tilting his head and stroking his chin, like he was really thinking about it. Then he leaned forward and drove a fist into the midsection of the gorilla costume. Burger dropped to his knees, making retching noises inside the costume. "Any more advice for me?" The semicircle of burly teenagers closed in.

"Just a minute!" Nick raised his hands and stepped in between the high schoolers and Burger. "Think about it. You have these illegal parties out here so that nobody catches you, right? Parents, cops, coaches—whatever."

"Exactly." Chet's voice was calm and reasonable. "Which is why little kids who spy on us get a beating. So nobody finds out."

"Oh, sure, I can see why that seems like a good plan. Of course." He nodded vigorously. "A beating would certainly have an impact. I would definitely not want to tattle, or ever spy on you again." Nick started to pace back in forth in front of his little audience, warming up.

"But think about it. I mean, it's not like you're going to actually *kill* us. We'll still be going home tonight. And if I'm all cut up or bruised—blood on my clothes or whatever—my mom is going to freak."

"So what?" Ox threw up his hands in exasperation. "If you tell her it was us, we'll just beat you again. Don't you get it?" He looked around at his buddies. "He seriously doesn't get it."

No, you don't get it. Nick stifled a smile. These guys were talking instead of punching. He'd already won. He just had to close the deal.

"Oh, I totally wouldn't want to tell. Obviously. I'm sure it would be a very thorough beating." Ox actually nodded in agreement, and Nick stifled another smile. That was another trick of negotiation: Have Your Opponent Commit to Little Yeses Before Getting the Big Yes.

"But my mom wouldn't listen to any made-up stories about how we got the injuries. She used to be a pediatric nurse. So she's been trained to tell the difference between a punch and a fall down the stairs." *A total lie, of course. But a few specific, believable details will convince people of almost anything.*

"And what's more, she knows we hang out in these woods after school." Nick walked back and forth in front of his audience like a defense attorney, ticking points off on his fingers. "She would march right down to the school to get to the bottom of it. And you know how they're having all of those stupid antibullying programs and assemblies this year? It's state law to have those things. And you know that's just so administrators can keep their jobs, am I right?"

Nick was in his element now, working his way through a logical argument. The confidence was evident in his voice. "So the principal would launch an investigation, and start leaning on people, interrogating everyone who comes down here. And somewhere, somehow, they'd find some loser who knows you guys have your keggers down here, but he's mad because he never gets invited. It's just like those cop shows; there's always a guy like that. So this loser—he'd rat you out. Anonymously, of course, but then you're dragged into it."

Nick risked a glance at the guys. Some of them were

definitely buying it. "And state law will require an immediate response. This antibullying initiative gets applied to everything, or else the schools open themselves up to lawsuits."

Nick shook his head in mock sadness and continued pacing. "So you know what that means: your coach gets involved. Sure, he doesn't want you guys to miss any games, not with the play-offs coming up. But you don't know my mom. She'll freak. She'll go to the newspaper, tell them to do a big story on how the bullies don't think the law applies to them."

Chet snorted. "Nobody cares what your mom says about—"

"And she'll bring pictures." Nick rushed along. "First thing pediatric nurses are trained to do. Get the evidence. Now, stuff like that isn't going to make the front page, but it'll make a nice little photo-op somewhere in the *Herald*'s sports blog. A couple of young kids all beat up, and then your football pictures right next to it. And once it gets in there, forget about it. Someone from Rivals.com picks it up and plasters it all over before the big game with Bellingham next week. The ugly side of social media. The pressure on your coach will be too much. He'll have to suspend you from the Bellingham game, and anything can happen with those cross-city rivalry matchups. Could seriously affect your seeding in the play-offs. You don't want to face Ferndale in the first round. Then your run's over before it really starts, you know?" Nick only paid attention to the sports pages for the betting odds —taking money from kids who picked teams based on heart rather than head was the easiest way to make a buck—but he was sure glad he had this information now.

Nick shrugged and held his hands palms up, a gesture that said he was helpless to fight the inevitable. "Yep, I'm afraid that if you beat us up, it's really going to come back and bite you. Look, I wouldn't tell. I promise. You have to believe that. But it would get out anyway. The team is undefeated, which means you guys are too high profile right now. Besides, your coach is going to wonder just what you're doing out here in the forest, anyway. And then you could lose your party place, too. Is it really worth all of that just to beat up a couple of kids?"

Nick could tell by the look on Chet's face that he would always answer yes to that question.

But Nick had gotten through to the others.

"Ah, let's go," the lean receiver said. "We have to get to practice."

"Yeah, this is a waste of time," muttered another guy.

Ox looked at Nick with an expression like he smelled something bad. "You're a weird kid."

The football team started tramping up the hill.

"Wait up," Chet called. They all turned at once. "At least get this costume off Fat Boy. Might come in handy at my little sister's party tomorrow."

Ox snorted. "Doesn't fit him anyway."

"They probably stole it." Chet slowly did pull-ups on his chair's roll bar while Ox unzipped the costume, yanked it off Burger's body, and threw it across his shoulder. "Smoke Valley kids can't afford a costume like that."

Chet slid back down into his seat, worked the armrest controls, and zipped to the head of the column of high schoolers, leading them up the trail and back to Chuckanut Drive.

Nick rubbed at his sore neck, finally able to breathe again. But it was probably more from relief than from not having Ox's fingers wrapped around his throat anymore.

Burger exhaled loudly and gave Nick a big, goofy grin. "Man, you're good at talking."

"Thanks for coming back and trying to save me from those guys," Nick said. "Even when the costume wasn't working."

"Not gonna lie, dude, I was pretty scared. I kept waiting for the gorilla powers to kick in, but the costume just felt different. I wonder what was up with that?"

Nick shrugged. "Who knows? But it's a good thing it doesn't work anymore. Can you imagine what would happen if Ox put that thing on?"

Burger shuddered and looked up the trail. "You know, it's probably a good thing the costume didn't work for me this time. It wouldn't be good for us to hurt Chet. Especially for you."

"What do you mean?"

"Come on, man. I'm not blind. I see the way you look at Hayley." Burger grinned. "Chet's going to be your brother-in-law someday."

"Oh, shut up." Nick's face got warm; he couldn't help it. He turned and marched down the trail. "Let's get going. We need to know if that grizzly costume is still occupied."

Washington State
Half an hour earlier

THE WORST THING ABOUT BEING A GRIZZLY WAS the itching. Chiggers, lice, caterpillars—it felt like the entire forest population was crawling all over his furry back. And there was no way to reach around there for a good scratch. Without opposable thumbs he couldn't just grab a branch and go to town. Now he understood why Baloo the bear was always raking his back against those cartoon trees in the old Disney movie.

Wait...maybe that would work for him? Thoughts seemed to be coming slower and slower to Connor the longer he had the bear costume on.

He wandered among the trees on all fours, enormous paws padding along on leaves and pine needles, until he found a nice, thick elm covered with rough bark. Perfect.

Connor placed the flat of his paws against the trunk for balance as he labored to stand on his hind legs. Turning around was the tricky part. He had to take dainty little bear steps in a circle. This body was not made for dainty. But eventually his back rested against the trunk.

He shifted his shoulders to move side to side, then bent his hind legs to go up and down. Ahhhhhh. It felt so good that he tried to do both of those things at the same time, really get a thorough scratch going. Ohhhh, that was nice. That was the nicest thing he'd felt since—

Crash! Connor slipped right off the tree. He lost his balance, staggered backward a few steps, and fell flat on his back in a tangle of bushes.

Connor dimly realized that he should probably feel embarrassed. But he didn't, not really. Maybe bears didn't get embarrassed. Why would they? They could just eat any woodland creatures that dared to laugh at them.

Wait—do animals laugh? Connor tried it, but a growly half roar came out instead. That struck him as funny, somehow, so he growled and chuckle-roared some more.

He stared up at the ceiling of intertwined branches overhead, the wet leaves dripping down on him. That felt nice. The cool mud felt good on his back, too. Just lying here, resting, was good. Natural. He felt like he could sleep for a month. He had been so busy for so long. When was the last time he just lay down and didn't think about anything?

Something tried to nag him at the back of his bear brain. There were things he was supposed to be worrying about, certainly. But as he lay on the forest floor, they grew a little fuzzy in his head. There was a truck, right? And something about a job he was supposed to do. But that didn't make sense. Bears didn't drive trucks. Or have jobs.

Maybe a little nap first. Later he could worry about—

The delivery! He remembered now. An important delivery. And a deadline. And a couple of boys that found him. The boys had been scared. Why had they been scared? Oh, probably because he was a bear. Right.

These things were important, he reminded himself, so important...

...although they didn't seem to have much to do with him. At least not at the moment. And he was so hungry. He realized that bears do have a job: eating things. How long had it been since he had eaten? Certainly before he visited his dad in the place with all the humans in the white coats. Hospital. It was called a hospital. And his dad was not a bear. That was weird.

But what was he supposed to do about his hunger? Bears ate fish, right? But not cooked. How could he make a fire when he could barely steer a truck? Was he supposed to just grab a big salmon out of a cold stream and shove it right in his mouth, chewing on the meat while the fish flopped around, alive and all?

The thought had sickened him at first. But now that he had been a bear for a few hours, it actually didn't sound that bad. He licked his black lips, imagining that fresh meat between his jaws, the blood dripping down his muzzle as he ripped and tore at the—

Rrrrrring!

Huh?

Rrrrrring! Rrrrrring!

He lurched upright until he was on his paws again. It was a phone; not a ring tone, but an old-fashioned phone ring. Something about the sound—so out of place here in the woods—pulled Connor back to himself. Made him remember that *he* was the one out of place in the woods.

Rrrrrring!

It was coming from the truck. He rushed back there, loping in between the trees, and found the back doors open.

More ringing. Connor stuck his head and shoulders into the back of the sideways truck. He craned his long neck forward and sniffed at the air. Seemed like the best way to start his search. But what did a phone smell like?

He switched tactics and pawed through the mess of costumes. His claws got stuck on a superhero cape. He shook his paw, trying to dislodge the satiny material, when the cape slipped to the side and revealed what was making the ringing sound.

It was a transparent sphere the size of a bowling ball. Connor recoiled so fast that his head smashed into the metallic side of the truck. Because within the clear ball was the head of that creepy woman from the forest. Mary Goodwin. And she did not look happy.

She was staring right at him and silently screaming, spittle flying everywhere and splattering the inside surface of the orb. Her bonnet slipped and sat lopsided on her head, and the hair that spilled out seemed to be flickering from blond to dull gray back to blond again. And that hermit-pale face had gone pink from all the exertion.

Rrrrrring!

He noticed that the sphere had been fused on top of an old-fashioned rotary phone. A crystal ball with long-distance service?

Connor reached out a paw and swiped at the receiver. It clattered onto the floor of the truck.

"—you thinking? I swear to the dark lord, I've never seen anything so stupid in all these years. And that's a lot of years, mister!" Her voice, a little tinny but plenty loud and shrill, came through the receiver. She jabbed a finger at him from inside the crystal ball. "You take that off right now. Hear me?" As her voice spiked in volume, her face did that melting thing, spilling down her cheeks in a waterfall of saggy wrinkles. She pushed them back into place and held them there until she looked young again. "You have any idea how hard it is to clean bear fur? This forest here don't exactly have a twenty-four-hour dry cleaners, you brainless newt."

Connor hung his furry head in shame.

"I'm not paying you to fiddle around with the merchandise. Got it? I call for an update and this is what I find?"

He tried to explain: Unpredictable wormholes. Scary moose. Magic costumes. A terrible crash. But all that came out was a pathetic little whimper-growl.

"Oh, save your breath, fur ball. Can't talk when you're in that getup." She pushed her face up against the glass of the ball and it went all fish-eyed and distorted. "Maybe you need a little incentive. Is that it? Maybe you don't even know the score."

She disappeared and Connor growl-sighed in relief. But she popped right back into view, this time holding a dented file box, rusted with age. Mary Goodwin rifled through the folders that were jammed in there and pulled out a yellowing piece of paper.

"You see this?" she snarled. "This is the deed to your folks' place. I bought that house for your family back in 1924. I could turn your mom out of there anytime I wanted." She snatched out another weathered sheet. "And this here belongs to the nursing home that's taken care of your family for generations. You got two sets of grandparents in there right now. How you think they'd fare on the streets?" She pulled out more and more forms. "Life insurance policies. Car titles. Retirement accounts."

She shook the wad of papers at him. "I've taken good care of your family for over three centuries." Mary Goodwin fixed him with a glare, the area around her eyes going wrinkly and gray in her anger. "But if you mess this up, I will ruin every living Flanagan overnight."

She reached back into the file box with a hand covered in liver spots. The skin was so thin that he could see every vein. "And that goes for you, too, mister." She pulled out another sheaf. "These look familiar? Student loans for that fancy dental school you go to. You honestly think your daddy could have afforded that school by delivering furniture or some such?" She held up the papers and made as if to rip them in half. "How'd you like to get kicked right out of that school and be stuck with the bill? And you with no job?"

Connor started whimpering. No wonder his dad had worked so hard and never complained. The fate of the entire extended Flanagan clan rested on the deliveryman's shoulders. And now on Connor.

Mary Goodwin took a deep breath and blinked hard. The wrinkles and liver spots disappeared and her hair shimmered and turned blond all over again. She primly stowed the papers back in the file box.

"*Ahem.* Do I have your attention now?"

Connor nodded his shaggy head.

She held up her fingers one at a time and ticked off a list: "Get that costume off. Make the delivery. Get back here. In that order." She set the box down and readjusted the bonnet on her head. "Better hope your little shenanigans haven't jeopardized this delivery," she said. "But if they have, remember the golden rule: destruction before detection. You'll be even deeper in debt to Mary Goodwin—oh, aye, that's for certain—but it'll be better than what happens to you—and your family—if you get caught."

He nodded his bear head again, wanting her to know he understood.

Then the crystal ball went dark.

12

"WHAT IS HE DOING?" NICK WHISPERED. HE AND
Burger were hiding behind a Douglas fir, watching the
bear drag a fallen birch sapling across the forest floor in
the fading daylight.

The grizzly shuffled backward on all fours, his jaws
clamped around the base of the young tree. Every few
steps, the log dropped from his mouth. Then he'd spit out
wood shavings with a sound like a cat hacking up a hair
ball, his tongue dripping a viscous slobber-and-tree-bark
slurry. After a quick shake of his head that looked like
an involuntary act of revulsion, he picked up the end of
the tree again.

"Is he trying to hide it, maybe?" The delivery truck
was half covered in logs and branches.

"You think?" Burger whispered. "He's not doing a very good job, then. Look at all the spaces between the big sticks."

"Wait a minute...." Nick studied the rough pattern the bear was making. The logs leaned against the truck vertically, circling the back end. Their thick bases were set at two-foot intervals around the truck, but their narrower ends met in the air; it looked like the skeletal supports for a tepee with the truck inside. Then Nick noticed several jumbles of smaller, tightly packed branches inside the logs. "It looks like he's getting ready for a bonfire. Maybe he wants to torch the whole thing."

"Whoa, you're right." Burger pushed the hair out of his eyes. "But why? If all of those costumes work—even if it's only one time—then that is the coolest truck in the history of the world."

"Maybe, but I don't think he's enjoying his costume experience." The bear retched up another wet ball of sawdust.

Burger took a deep breath. "Well? You ready to make contact?"

"I guess." A tangle of nerves swarmed in Nick's belly. "But what if we're wrong and it's a real bear?"

Burger shrugged. "I don't know, then we'll climb a tree or something. Maybe we could even—"

"ROO–OOAA–AR!"

Burger jumped in surprise and cracked his head on a low-hanging branch. Nick scooped up a rock and got into a defensive crouch. They both peered around the tree trunk.

The grizzly was swaying on his hind legs next to the delivery truck. He gripped the birch sapling awkwardly in his front paws, trying to prop it up, but half of the other logs had fallen down. The bear's carefully constructed tepee structure lay in ruins.

He let the log fall out of his paws and slumped down on all fours with a dispirited half roar. Then the bear leaned forward and *bonked* his head against the truck. Nick thought it was just more of the beast's clumsiness, but the grizzly lifted his head and let it drop again. *Bonk.* And again.

Bonk.

Bonk.

Bonk.

His head carved out a dent on the side of the truck.

"Whatever that thing is, it needs some help," Nick said. After all, he did feel responsible for this truck ending up in the middle of the woods. And he couldn't help but wonder what it would have been like if he were permanently stuck inside that robot. How long would it take to get totally lost in one of those costumes? To actually stop being yourself? Nobody deserved that. So even though he was still plenty nervous, Nick moved from behind the tree and into the small clearing to help the grizzly. Burger followed.

Nick cleared his throat. The bear must not have heard

over the sound his skull made as it slammed against metal.

Nick took a deep breath. "Hey!" he yelled. "Over here!"

The bear whirled around, first one way, then the other, like a dog chasing its own tail. His wide eyes scanned the forest.

Finally he saw the boys and became very still. His shaggy head swiveled slowly to look at the truck, and then back to regard the boys again. He did this a few times before taking a couple of cautious steps forward. But when the boys shrank back against the tree, he stopped moving completely and simply watched.

"I have an idea," Burger said.

Nick tightened his grip on the rock, scoped out an escape route. He had seen Burger's ideas in action before.

Burger stepped a little farther into the clearing. He pointed at the truck, then at the bear, and finally at himself. Then he started pacing back and forth, whistling, as if he didn't have a care in the world.

What is he doing? Nick wondered.

Burger stopped and pretended to see something on the ground, his face stretching into an exaggerated expression of surprise. Then he elaborately pantomimed picking something big up off the forest floor and putting it on, first the legs and then the arms.

Oh, no way. He's trying to play charades with the bear.

After Burger had his invisible "costume" on, he roared and shambled around on all fours like a bear. Then he abruptly stood up, pointed to the bear, then at himself, and finally pantomimed unzipping a costume from neck to navel.

The bear sat back on his furry haunches and tilted his head, staring at Burger.

"Why are you doing that?" Nick stage-whispered.

"I'm communicating with the bear. Duh."

"But you could hear perfectly well in the gorilla suit. So why not just talk to it?"

"Oh. Right."

"Duh." Nick elbowed past Burger to face the bear. He called out, "If you can understand me, raise your right paw."

Slowly, the grizzly raised one of its hairy mitts.

"Awesome!" said Burger, a goofy grin lighting up his face in the gloom of forest twilight. "We're actually talking to a bear. And he understands!"

"That's his *left* paw. I guess neither of you geniuses noticed."

The bear snorted and shook his head, then dropped the paw and raised the other one.

Nick took another small step forward. "Are you stuck inside one of those costumes?"

The grizzly turned to look at the back of the truck again, and then scanned the forest all around them, as if checking for eavesdroppers. Then he faced Nick and nodded his massive head.

"Do you need us to try and get you out?" Burger said.

A pause. The bear tried to chew on his lower lip. Then another nod. The beast leaned forward on all fours and shuffled toward the boys.

"Wait," Nick whispered out the side of his mouth. "What if he's only doing this to draw us in? And then he eats us?"

Burger snorted. "Dude. Then that bear is the greatest predator of all time. He'd *deserve* to eat us."

The grizzly closed to within five yards of Burger. He leaned forward, stretching out his neck and offering it to the boy.

Yikes. Those shoulders alone were bigger than Burger's entire body. Seeing his friend that close to the bear's mouth was unnerving. He inched closer, tightening his grip on the rock, ready to step up if that thing lunged at his friend.

Burger reached underneath the grizzly's jaw and his hands disappeared inside brown fur. He moved his hands back and forth, frowning in concentration, then ducked down for a better look. But it was an awkward position, hunching over and looking up at the same time.

He continued to search. The bear stared off into the middle distance like a bored patient waiting for the dentist to quit fumbling around with the drill and get on with it, already.

"I don't think that's working," Nick said. He met the bear's eyes. "Hey, think you can stand on two legs? That might help."

The bear shakily raised himself up on his hind legs and towered over Burger, who craned his neck to stare up at the grizzly. "Okay, there's no way I can reach it now." Burger looked over his shoulder at Nick. "Give me a boost."

Nick shook his head. "You weigh twice as much as I do."

Burger shrugged. "Then I'll give you a boost."

Nick looked up at the beast, a mini-mountain covered in fur. There must be another, non-Burger way to do this. "I don't know...."

The grizzly snorted impatiently and dropped back to all fours. Then he leaned down and rolled over on his back, legs in the air, a submissive puppy waiting to have his tummy rubbed.

"Thanks, my man." The boys knelt beside the bear's neck and combed their fingers through the fur. Nick could feel the animal's warm breath on his arms. The softness of the fur surprised him as he tried to find the end of the zipper. "Wait, I think I got it."

"Nice!" Burger said. "Unzip it."

"It's stuck." Nick yanked on the zipper.

"Here, let me help."

"No, your hands are too big. I'll lose my grip." Nick shoved at Burger with his free hand. "Get away. I can do it."

Burger positioned himself behind Nick and grabbed him around the chest.

"What are you doing?"

"Just hold the zipper tight," Burger said. He was jostling around, trying to get solid footing on the wet ground next to the bear. "Count to three, keep a strong grip, and then I'll pull you backward and—"

ROOO-AAA-OOAR!

Those enormous jaws snapped open and flecks of hot bear spit splattered Nick's face. The boys scurried backward and landed in a heap on the wet ground. Nick instinctively wrapped himself up into a ball, hands over his head, waiting for one of those gigantic paws to land a deathblow.

A few terrifying moments stretched out.

Finally: "Sorry, dude."

Nick opened one eye to find Burger standing, holding up both hands in front of the bear in a calming gesture. "It was just an accident, big fella."

The bear glared at Burger but lay down on his back again. "What happened?" Nick said.

Burger whispered behind his hand. "I think I stepped right on . . . you know, on his bear business."

Nick rolled his eyes. "Well, be careful. My head was practically in his mouth."

The boys got into position again. Nick gripped the zipper, counted to three, and both boys pulled as hard as they could.

The zipper came unstuck and ran down the length of the bear's body. All of that fur fell away.

The guy who jumped out was long and gangly with a mop of fiery red hair and a face full of freckles to match. Faded blue coveralls hung loosely off his scrawny frame. He swallowed heavily, his knobby Adam's apple bobbing up and down.

He raised his hands in front of his face, slowly flexing them open and closed, probably making sure they weren't paws. After a sigh of relief, he closed his eyes and murmured, "Oh, thank you so much."

Then his eyes flew open and he reached out and clamped a hand on each boy's shoulder.

"You kids got a lighter?"

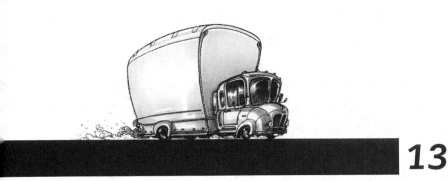

13

EVEN THOUGH HE HAD MORE THAN HALF EXPECTED it to happen, Nick was still a little rattled by seeing some guy jump out of the belly of a grizzly bear. And now that guy was staring at them so intently, his green eyes wide and more than a little wild.

But he had to keep it together. They needed to figure out what was going on. Nick swallowed his fear and stuck his hand out. The guy just stared at it. Nick pressed on anyway. "Hello. My name is—"

"A lighter. Do you have one? I gotta get my hands on one right away."

"Gotcha covered," Burger said. He dug an orange Bic out of his jeans pocket. "I like to burn stuff sometimes."

"I need that." The lanky redhead lunged at the lighter,

but Burger whisked it away. The guy made another grab, but Burger backpedaled and held it behind his back at arm's length.

"Not so fast! Why do you need it so bad?"

The guy froze while his eyes scanned the forest again, as if he thought they were being watched. He wiped sweat beads off his forehead. Nick thought he looked like he might burst into tears at any moment.

When he spoke again, it was in a strangled whisper. "Who have you told? About the truck?" Those big green eyes went back and forth between the two boys.

"No one." Nick shook his head. The guy's eyes narrowed in suspicion. "Seriously."

"We promise," Burger said.

"What about...you know..." He stretched out a long arm to indicate the bear costume lying lifeless in the mud.

The boys looked at each other. "Well..."

"*What?* What happened?"

"There are these high school guys," Nick said. "And they sort of grabbed one of the costumes from us."

"A gorilla," Burger added.

The redhead covered his face in his hands and slumped down on a log, moaning "No," over and over.

"But it's okay!" Nick said. Man, this guy was really freaked out. "Don't worry. It's going to be okay."

"How?" The guy kept his face covered up. "How is it possibly going to be okay?"

"These guys, they don't know about the special

powers," Burger said. "And that costume's not working anymore, anyway."

The guy lifted his head up at that, eyebrows furrowed in confusion. "Really?"

"Yeah, maybe we used up all of its powers, or whatever. See, we put them on, and then we had this fight in the backyard—not a real fight, just playin'—and then we tried to—"

Nick kicked Burger to get him to shut up. The guy's face was just looking more and more worried as Burger kept talking.

"It doesn't matter how it happened. Just believe us—that costume's not working anymore," Nick said. "Don't even worry about it."

The redhead shook his head as if to clear it and then stood back up. "Okay. Give me the lighter. Then run away. Get out of here." He stretched out his palm, but Burger didn't move. "And, um, don't ever come back or whatever. And don't say anything to anybody about what you saw. Just forget all about it. Or else, you know, I'll, uh . . . I'll do something bad to you." He cleared his throat. "Real bad."

The boys remained motionless. The redhead sighed deeply again.

"Please?"

Burger kept the lighter behind his back. "If you're going to torch that truck, then no way."

The guy drew himself up straighter and stuck his

meager chest out. "All right. If that's how it is, I'll just have to take it from you, then."

Burger grunted out a half laugh. "No offense, dude, but you were way scarier as a bear."

"Oh, yeah? Well, I'm way older than you, and I'm not about to let a couple of kids—"

A crow cawed somewhere nearby in the forest. The guy let out a little shriek and spun around, scanning the trees.

Nick and Burger looked at each other, trying not to smirk. The guy collected himself, lifting his head higher and flattening out the creases in his coveralls.

"Look, whatever's the matter, maybe we can help, okay?" Nick left the words *for a fifty-fifty split of the profit* unspoken. No sense starting a negotiation before you knew the score. "We don't even know your name. I'm Nick, and this is Burger."

The guy stopped, the costume dangling from his grip. "Connor. Flanagan," he said, studying them. "You're the kids on the bikes."

A wave of shame burned red patches on Nick's cheeks. "We are so sorry about that."

"No. It's not your fault. It's mine. Like everything else." Connor gazed into the middle distance, silent, his thoughts clearly elsewhere.

Nick finally said, "Okay, now we know each other's names. So . . . what are you doing out there?"

The guy watched them warily, drawing out the silence even longer, before he said, "The less you know, the better."

"Come on. We're totally trustworthy and stuff."

The guy shook his head and that mop of bright red hair flopped around. "Look, take my word on this. *Please.* It's better if I burn the whole thing and just get out of here."

"But why?" Nick and Burger said it at the same time.

"Because if I get caught with these, she's going to ruin my entire family." When the gangly figure in the coveralls studied the boys, it seemed like the first time he was actually seeing them. "And apparently we've known her for years. I can only imagine what she would do to you two."

14

CONNOR FLANAGAN HURRIED BACK TO THE TRUCK
and began frantically restacking the logs. Nick and Burger
glanced at each other, eyebrows raised in a mutual question, before they followed.

"Who?" Nick asked when they reached the truck.
"Why?" But the guy wordlessly strained to lift another
log and worry it into position, his work boots slipping
across the soft ground. "Who would try to ruin you?"

Connor kept about his business, grunting with effort.
Burger stepped in between him and the next log he was
about to pick up.

Finally Connor stopped and looked at the boys. "You
don't want me to tell you."

"Why not?"

"I told you—you'd be next on her list."

While the boys thought about that one, the guy hunched over, grabbed a log, and backed his way over to the truck. But in his haste he nudged one of the standing logs with his hip, and the remaining half of the tepee structure collapsed like dominoes, hitting the ground in a series of wet thuds.

He stood up and surveyed the wreckage, a bleak look in his eyes. Then he shuffled closer to the truck, raised his eyes to the sky—Nick thought maybe he was praying —and then let his head fall against a dirty panel. *Bonk.* And again. *Bonk.*

"Whoa, not that again." Nick rushed to his side and pulled Connor away from the truck.

He whirled around and pointed at Burger. "Then tell him to give me the lighter. It's the only way." His desperate voice cracked on the last word, and Nick was sure that he really was going to start crying this time.

Nick shook his head. "You realize that if the truck catches fire, it's going to hit the gas tank and explode, right? And that could cause a forest fire. Even with the trees still damp from all the rain."

Connor slumped against the trunk as if he had lost the will to remain upright. He ended up sitting in a crumpled heap on the forest floor, head buried in his hands.

"You're right," he moaned. "Oh, why did I ever get stuck with this crazy job in the first place?" He shook his head fiercely and scrubbed his hair with both hands in frustration, making it stick up all over, Einstein-style.

The boys stood there in awkward silence, glancing off into the forest. What were you supposed to do when some guy was having a nervous breakdown or whatever right in front of you?

Connor snuffled and groaned. He muttered a few things the boys didn't understand. Finally he fell silent.

After he had just sat there for a few minutes, hugging his knees to his chest, Nick dropped to the ground and sat cross-legged in front of him. Burger followed suit.

"Let's start with the start," Nick said. "You're not from around here, right?"

After a few quiet moments, Connor shook his head without looking up. It was at least something, Nick thought.

"No problem," Burger said. "We know every inch of this place. I'm telling you, man, we can help."

When the guy offered no protest, verbal or otherwise, Nick continued. "So these costumes. They're pretty special, obviously. And I guess you're trying to keep them a secret?"

A pause. Then a nod.

"Do you make 'em?" Burger blurted out. "How? Are they magic? For reals? Where'd you learn how to do that? How much do they—"

Nick punched Burger in the shoulder to shut him up

and pointed to the guy, who was shaking his head, but just barely.

"Okay, you don't make the costumes, but you're driving around in a truck full of them," Nick said. "Soooo... what? You must be taking them somewhere. Are you, like, delivering them or something?"

Pause. Another nod.

"Now we're getting somewhere." Burger rubbed his hands together. "Where are you taking them?"

Connor continued to stare at the ground. "I can't tell you that," he finally croaked. "Oh, I'm no good at this. Why did he ever think I'd be any good at this?"

Burger leaned forward eagerly. "Who? Who thought you'd be—"

"No," the guy groaned. "I've said too much. Just leave me alone." His already-slumped body folded in on itself even further. He rocked back and forth in a little ball, softly moaning to himself.

Burger jumped to his feet and crossed his arms over his chest. Nick saw his face sprout purple blotches of frustration and knew his friend was about to have a blowup of some kind. "You wanna be that way? Fine! Then we'll just take—"

Nick grabbed Burger's arm and made a slashing motion across his throat. Burger glared sideways at his friend. Nick mouthed the words *"Trust me."*

Would the Takeaway work on adults the same way it

worked on the clueless rich kids back at school? Maybe. But he'd have to really sell it.

Nick backed away several steps. "All right. We'll leave, if that's what you really want," he called to Connor. He took a few more steps away. "But good luck getting a fire going without a lighter. Burger and I tried the rubbing-two-sticks-together thing before. Did it for hours. All we ended up with was a couple of smooth sticks."

"Yeah. And blisters," Burger said.

Nick kept backing up and made a *follow-me* gesture to Burger. "And have fun camping out here after dark. We've done it lots of times, but never, you know, without supplies or gear or anything. It gets really cold around here after sunset."

The stranger didn't budge.

Nick tried again, raising his voice as they got farther away. "Oh, and be sure to keep that bear costume handy. You might need it in case the real thing shows up in the middle of the night. Maybe you could trick it, scare it off or something. I hear they like to carbo-load right before hibernation. Burger and I've seen all kinds of bears out here."

Burger crinkled up his eyebrows. "No, we haven't. There's no—"

Nick kicked Burger in his meaty leg and glared at him, gesturing at the comatose form slumped in front of the truck.

A light of realization dawned in Burger's eyes. "Oh, yeah. Ri-i-ight. You should listen to my friend here. The bears are really aggressive in these parts." He dropped an exaggerated wink at Nick. "Getting that costume back on is a good idea for your own protection . . . you just better hope it's not mating season. You were a pretty cute bear." Burger raised his eyebrows and made a *did-I-do-good?* face at Nick.

Was the guy finally stirring? It looked like maybe he was trying to peek out at the boys from behind that screen of red hair.

Nick deliberately turned his back and strode away from the clearing. "Oh, and a big wolf costume might come in handy if you've got one stashed back there," he called out over his shoulder. "I think we're in the middle of the pack's hunting grounds. Those guys are pretty territorial."

Burger caught up with Nick and matched his strides. "Yeah," he yelled, a little too loudly. "And don't forget about all of the raccoons."

"What are you doing?" Nick whispered fiercely. "Raccoons aren't scary."

"They weird me out, dude," Burger whispered back. "They just sit there and stare at you, wringing their hands to show off their little opposable thumbs. It's creepy."

The boys continued to march away.

Burger cleared his throat. "But what if he doesn't—"

"Trust me."

They took a few more steps before:

"Wait."

Nick and Burger spun around. Connor dug through a pocket of his coveralls and held up a piece of paper.

The boys rushed back and Burger snatched the paper. "What's this?"

The guy was still looking at the ground. "The address. Where I'm supposed to deliver the costumes."

Nick and Burger looked at the paper and then at each other, eyebrows raised. They recognized the address; it belonged to a mansion right on the bay, pretty close to Hayley's house. But this place was at the end of a private, gated road that broke off from Chuckanut Drive and led down to a secluded cove.

"You know where that is?" the guy said.

"Yeah. I think these people are super rich," Burger said.

"They'd have to be, to afford this shipment." Connor looked up again and stared at them with those green eyes. Then he stuck out his hand.

Nick grabbed the guy's hand and helped pull him to his feet.

Connor studied the boys for another moment and then exhaled loud and long. "Before you decide to help me, I need to tell you the whole story."

Nick nodded. "Cool."

"But you have to swear yourselves to secrecy." He

looked down and dusted off his coveralls before fixing the boys with his gaze again. "I don't even really know the whole story myself. But from what I can tell, you'd be the only outsiders who have found out for hundreds of years."

PART III

THE
DELIVERY

15

NICK SAT ON TOP OF THE TRUCK, WRITING ON AN
envelope salvaged from the glove box while Burger and
Connor Flanagan gathered up the pile of spilled costumes
and folded them back into garment boxes.

"Hey, look at this one!" Burger stepped out of the cargo
bay and held up a furry costume with a ferocious lion's
head. "One of us could slip this on at the zoo and run
all over the place. The other one could run out in front
screaming, '*The lion has escaped!*' and freak people out.
How fun would that be?"

Nick nodded but barely looked up. Burger interrupted
him every minute or so with a new plan to terrorize the
citizens of Bayside.

"Whoa, or how about these?" Burger showed off a

couple of scaly costumes, maybe velociraptors. "You know that dinosaur exhibit at the museum? What if we put these on, hid in there with the dino-mannequins, and stayed real still, then jumped out right in the middle of an elementary school field trip? How bad would that freak people out?"

Nick nodded again with a noncommittal grunt, eyes still fixed on the paper. He was almost finished.

Connor sighed in exasperation. "Come on, kid, just help me get the costumes back in these boxes and stacked up." He pulled one of the oversize reptile costumes from Burger's grip and folded it, scanning the surrounding woods with a worried look on his face.

Nick set his pencil down and double-checked the figures. Everything looked good.

"Oh, no way, this would be the best. The absolute best." Burger held up a dark cape in one hand and a pair of fangs in the other. "We could go to one of those lame movies where the vampires are always kissing people instead of drinking their blood and then they talk about their *feelings* for two hours. And then, right at the most boring part, we could put these on, and jump out growling and snapping. Remind people that vampires are supposed to actually be scary. Total freak-out, guaranteed."

"Sure, Burger. Whatever." Nick jumped down from the truck and approached Connor Flanagan. "Okay, here it is. If you'd like our help, I think this document adequately outlines a fair compensation package."

```
20-foot U-Haul truck rental
  (24 hours)............................. $39.95
Additional U-Haul fee:
  .79 per mile x 20 miles............... $15.80
Tank of gas ............................. $75
Fee for stealthy acquisition of truck .. $200
Hourly rate of pay:
  $20 (x 2 workers x 6 hours) ......... $240
Hazard pay:
  $20 (x 2 workers x 6 hours) ......... $240
Confidentiality agreement............. $250 (x 2 = $500)
Insurance against detection ........... $200
Total:................................ $1,510.75
```

Connor gulped. "You want me to pay you fifteen hundred bucks to help me out?"

"Fifteen hundred and ten dollars and seventy-five cents."

"But, wait, weren't you the ones who forced me off the road in the first place? I wouldn't even need your help if not for—"

"Dude, you were a bear." Burger threw the last box into the back of the truck. "You needed lots of help."

"Besides, I already factored in a discount based on our culpability." Nick pointed to the makeshift envelope-contract. "It would be way more expensive otherwise. Plus, you'll note that some of that fee goes straight to expenses."

Connor shook his head and stared at the paper. "What *are* some of these things, anyway...hazard pay?"

"Working outdoors. Inclement weather. Wild animals. Mysterious cargo." Nick shrugged. "It's not your usual after-school job."

"Insurance against detection?"

"Oh, yeah." Burger stepped forward. "We'll make sure nobody finds you down here."

"But...but...I don't have that kind of money to just give you." Connor exhaled heavily. When he waved the paper at Nick, his hands were shaking. "I don't have *any* kind of money right now, to be honest."

Walked right into that one. Perfect. "Well...we might be able to work something out."

Connor gulped. "Like what?"

"If you split the overall proceeds with us fifty-fifty, then we assume all risk and up-front expenses." Nick had already figured that this would amount to much more than he was asking for on his itemized list. Plus, it's not like they'd be asking this guy to pay for anything out-of-pocket. Whoever he was working for—someone who had the power and capital to make these incredible costumes —*that's* where the real money was.

Man, he'd never had a score close to this big before. Maybe...he hardly dared even dream it, but there was a chance his mom would be able to quit one of her jobs. How cool would it be to pay the rent on their place for a year and she wouldn't even have to worry about it. And if they did a good enough job, he bet this guy would let them help out with other deliveries. Now that he and Burger knew the big secret, if they showed they could be trusted, this could turn into something big for both of them.

"Fine. Fifty percent of the proceeds. I'll do it."

No negotiation or anything. Almost takes the fun out of it. Nick nodded. "Okay, you got yourself a—"

"And two costumes," Burger blurted out. "We each want to be able keep one of the costumes. The kind that won't quit working after one time."

Nick was ready to be annoyed with Burger, but he had to admit it was a pretty good idea. If his mom only had to go to one job *and* she had a robot-housekeeper? She'd feel like one of the Bayside Garden socialites.

Connor looked at the ground. "Oh, I don't know ... that's not up to me, you know? You'd have to ask ... you know ..."

He couldn't even say the name of that creepy lady in the woods. Nick didn't blame him—even Burger had gotten spooked during that part of the story.

"We can worry about that later, okay?" Nick said. "After the job's done, you'll be able to relax, and she'll probably be so grateful that it worked out that it'll be easier to ask her." Besides, Nick thought, after forcing Connor off the road, they owed him some help, money or not. Plus, he seemed like a good guy. Not everyone would have trusted a couple of kids with a secret this big no matter how bad a fix they were in. "We'll help you out."

Connor's face lightened with relief for a moment, before quickly twisting up with worry again. "So I guess that means you'll be leaving now?" He glanced nervously around the forest. It was getting pretty dark.

"We'll be back tomorrow, fully equipped to make the delivery. After we park the U-Haul up on the road, we'll hike down here and help you carry the costumes up. It should take a few hours to get them all loaded, but then it's a short drive to the drop-off. You'll have plenty of time to make your delivery. Easy." *And half of that money will be in our pockets by tomorrow afternoon.*

"But then how will I get back home?"

Burger gestured toward the truck "Your rig's in great shape for being in such a nasty wreck. That must be part of its special powers that lady was telling you about, right? Not only can it go through wormies or whatever—"

"Wormholes," Nick corrected.

"—but it looks like it's indestructible, too." Burger walked over and patted one of the upturned tires. "So you just go back the same way you came."

"He's right," Nick said. "After you make the delivery and all of the costumes are gone, then it'll be safe to get the authorities involved. We call in the wreck and the police help you get towed to the top."

"Through the woods? I don't see how—"

"Or wait! I bet they get one of those heavy-duty cargo helicopters and airlift this thing out. How cool would that be? Do you think they'd let us ride in it? Do you think we could sit up front and watch the—"

"Let's figure that out after the delivery, okay, Burger?" Nick pulled his friend away from the truck and toward the trail. "We really need to get going—it'll be totally dark pretty soon."

Burger took off his jacket and handed it to Connor. "Stay warm, dude."

"Thank you." Connor Flanagan looked like he might start to cry again. That guy had had a rough day. "Are you sure you're going to be able to get a U-Haul?" he said. "They don't rent to kids, you know. And I don't need to remind you that you are sworn to secrecy, so you can't pull anyone else into this plan—"

Nick held up his hands. "Look, you're welcome to go get the U-Haul while we stay here and guard the costumes."

Connor bit his lip and looked from the truck to the surrounding trees. His eyes were both wild and focused inward, like he was remembering something very unpleasant. "I can't leave the costumes." It came out in a whisper.

"Okay, then trust us. We'll take care of it."

"But how?"

"I'm glad you asked. It turns out we *will* need a

little help. Burger, did you find something that might be useful?"

Burger grinned and held up two garment boxes.

Nick looked at Connor. "It's strictly for business purposes, of course. But we'll be taking a couple of costumes with us."

16

NICK AND BURGER HUDDLED BEHIND THE GAZEBO in the town park. The drizzle had dried up and a bright moon peeked out between drifting clouds.

Despite his excitement, Nick had to stifle a yawn. They had pretended to be sleeping over at Burger's house and snuck out after midnight to ride their bikes into town.

"This is gonna be so awesome." Burger opened one of the garment boxes and pulled out a very thin piece of fabric. It was flimsier than gauze and mostly transparent. The only way Nick could tell that Burger was holding anything at all was when the moonlight caught the material and it shimmered.

"So you really think that's an Invisible Man costume?" Nick whispered.

"Totally. Check it out." Burger wrapped the flimsy material around his forearm and everything below his elbow disappeared.

Burger kicked off his shoes and started pulling his shirt over his head.

"Wait—what are you doing?"

"It doesn't do any good to be invisible if you're wearing clothes!"

"Oh, great, I didn't even think about that. So you're going to be a *naked* Invisible Man. That's disgusting." Nick backed up a few steps. "Just try the costume on first. If it works, and you're invisible, you can take your clothes off then."

"Whatever."

Burger threw the transparent sheet over his head. He disappeared and his clothes fell to the ground in a crumpled heap.

"Wow, you were really in a hurry to get those clothes off."

No answer. Nick turned in a circle, eyes darting all around. "Burger? Where are you?" He cautiously waved his hand through the air over the pile of clothes. Nothing. "Burger, this isn't funny."

"BOO!" The sound exploded right by Nick's ear, followed by laughter as he jumped in surprise and wheeled around, hands sweeping blindly out in front of him.

"Not cool," Nick said after he calmed down. "Where are you?"

"Right here."

Nick gasped as something poked him in the chest.

"Can you really not see me?" Poke in the shoulder. Poke on the stomach. Poke. Poke. Poke.

"Stop it!" Nick squinted. There was a single lightbulb behind the gazebo, and he thought maybe he could see something shimmering in the air, like heat waves floating above the freeway on a summer day. "Okay, we need to figure out if it affected your strength or anything. I could feel the pokes, but can you lift something? Try that can."

A Coke can rose up from the ground and hovered in midair. Then it twirled around a few times. Then it crumpled inward until it was a smashed disc. Then it flew forward and clunked Nick in the forehead. "No problem."

"Knock it off." Nick rubbed his head. "All right, let's try something heavier...can you pick up your bike?"

Nick watched the bike, but it didn't move. "I have a better idea." The voice came from behind him. All of a sudden the back of Nick's sweatshirt was hiked up, two unseen hands got a grip on the elastic band of his underwear, and his shorts were pulled up painfully. Mercilessly.

"Invisible wedgie!"

"Will you stop it?" Nick wheeled around, striking out with his fists but hitting nothing.

The laughter swirled around him. "That's hilarious! We have to give Chet an invisible wedgie. And all his friends. Just think how perfect that would be."

"The costumed-revenge thing didn't really work out for you the last time you tried it with those guys."

"Whatever. Will you get your costume on now? Let's go get that truck."

Nick took a deep breath, opened the second box, and threw the thin material over his head.

"Whoa," Burger said.

"What's going on?" Now that Nick had the costume on, he could see Burger. His friend wasn't naked, or at least if he was, Nick (thankfully) couldn't really tell. His form was a bluish-white flowing mound, and it was hard to determine where, exactly, his body stopped and the night began; the edges sort of flickered. But that was definitely Burger's smiling face on top.

"Wait—why can we see each other?" Burger said. "We're both supposed to be invisible, right?"

"I know. It doesn't make any sense." Nick looked Burger up and down. "You look blobbier than usual." Nick noticed that his clothes were also in a pile on the ground. "I don't remember taking my clothes off," he said.

Burger frowned. "That's weird...neither do I. Just seemed natural to have them off."

Normally, Nick would have thought that was a weird thing to say. But these were not normal times. Besides, he could sort of relate to what Burger was saying. Who needed clothes?

Burger tilted his head. "What's that noise?"

Nick listened. It sounded like a party in the streets.

The same streets that had been nearly empty just a minute ago.

The boys peeked around the edge of the gazebo and looked down the main street through town.

"Whoa."

Bluish-white forms, glowing as if lit from within, were all over the place. Gliding down the street, resting on benches, gazing into the shop windows…

"What's going on?"

"Why are there invisible people all over the place?"

"There's no way they could have found the costumes. Just not possible."

Nick backed up a few steps. "What do we…should we hide?"

"Dude!"

"What?"

"Look over there." Burger pointed down the street. "Doesn't that look like Mrs. Monahan?"

"No way." Nick squinted. "Didn't she die last spring?"

"Yeah, she must have been a hundred. At least."

"She doesn't seem to be a hundred now." Indeed, Mrs. Monahan was floating quickly down the street, laughing, arm in arm with a bluish-white gentleman.

She spotted them standing on the sidewalk and glided right over. "Hello, boys!" she said before Nick and Burger could run away.

Mrs. Monahan floated up to them, pulling her friend along with her. "Why, I recognize you two." Nick remembered the old lady as a mostly inert lump that sat on her porch and only mustered up enough energy to scowl when their bike wheels touched her lawn. Nothing like the radiant, smiling face before them now.

Burger's eyes got wide. "This is too weird," he whispered to Nick out the side of his mouth.

Mrs. Monahan inclined her head toward the floating man-shape beside her. "May I introduce you to Mr. Draper?"

He bowed. "The dapper Mr. Draper, if you please."

"Mr. Draper?" Nick said. "Wasn't that the name of the guy—"

"—who got hit by the train last month?" Burger's mouth hung open.

"The one and only!" Mr. Draper said, smiling. "I left the nursing home for a nice walk around the grounds that morning and must have gotten a bit disoriented. I'm afraid I didn't have all my faculties about me at the end there."

"So that means that you two are...actually..." For some reason Nick couldn't make himself say the word *ghosts*.

"Of course, sweetie." Mrs. Monahan leaned toward them. "So, how did you two let go?"

Nick and Burger looked at each other. "Let go?"

The guy's bushy, bluish-white mustache twitched as he smiled. "That's right. You know, cross the River Styx?

Rage against the dying of the light? Shuffle off the ol' mortal coil?"

"He means die," Mrs. Monahan said. "You'll have to forgive Mr. Draper. He was an English professor *before*, and now he has all the time he wants to revisit the classics."

Mr. Draper waggled his bushy, ghostly eyebrows. "You're the classic I'm most interested in revisiting, my dear." He leaned over and kissed Mrs. Monahan on her cheek. And she giggled. Actually giggled. Then kissed him back.

Nick and Burger looked at each other again. This was *way* grosser than any haunted house.

"So, what was it, my dears?" Mrs. Monahan said.

"Yes, how did you come to join us in the afterlife?"

"Oh!" Nick said. "No, we're not dead."

Mrs. Monahan clucked her tongue and shook her head. "Oh, my. Well, that's what they all say at first, isn't it?"

"It can be a lot to take in. An adjustment, certainly," Mr. Draper said.

"But you'll soon grow to love it."

The ex-people that flowed by on the sidewalk certainly seemed to be enjoying it. Like Mrs. Monahan, most of them had been old when they died, but they seemed buoyant and carefree now. Across the street on the park lawn, a group of ghosts was ballroom-dancing, gliding along without ever quite touching the grass and doing little air tricks as they dipped and twirled.

"No, seriously, we're not dead," Nick said.

Mrs. Monahan tsk-tsked. "Boys, please. I have seen the way you raced your bikes around in the middle of the street. Let's be honest, it was only a matter of time before you joined us."

"Is it always like this?" Burger stared at the ghost party raging across the streets of Bayside. "All of . . . them . . . out there?"

"Oh, yes," the dapper and deceased Mr. Draper said. "For a while they try to make contact with the living—"

"It's a phase; we all go through it. You will, too," Mrs. Monahan said.

"—but everyone settles into this new plane of existence pretty quickly. And soon you won't feel like paying the living any mind."

"To be honest, you quickly realize that they're dreadfully boring. Life is wasted on the living, is what we say. So fixated on time and dates and jobs and *things*."

"When there are much better pursuits to be fixated on." Mr. Monahan leaned over and stole another kiss from a giggling Mrs. Monahan.

Ugh. Time to go.

"Um, it was nice to see you again, Mrs. Monahan, but we have to get going. We, you know, have some stuff to do."

"Haven't quite got the hang of it yet, have they?" Mrs. Monahan smiled. "Ah, well. No matter. They will soon learn that the pressure of having *stuff to do* is a thing of the past. Enjoy the sweet hereafter, boys!"

"Good luck to you both. I'm sure we'll be seeing you again!" With that Mr. Draper whisked Mrs. Monahan down the street, both of them floating and smiling. They approached the library at the end of the street...and then glided right through the brick wall by the entrance, arm in arm.

"Dude." Burger shuddered, his shimmering form flickering all over. "I don't know about this."

"About what?"

"That gorilla costume—the longer I stayed in it, the more I became like a real gorilla, you know?"

"Yeah...?"

"Well, I don't want to become a *real* dead person! That's too creepy. What if we can't change back? What if it's not that easy?" A panicked look came to Burger's eyes. "In fact, I'm taking this thing off right now." He hunched over and grabbed at his shoulders, tugging upward.

"Stop it!" Nick floated over and pushed Burger's hands away. "The costume might not work again if you take it off, remember? Come on. We have a job to do."

"Do you seriously want the money that bad?"

Nick sighed. "It's not just that. Not anymore. We kind of owe it to Connor, you know? I mean, we did force that truck off the road. If he didn't swerve right off the cliff, we could actually be *real* ghosts right now."

Burger nodded. "Yeah, that's a good point."

"Plus, the poor guy just lost his dad last night." Nick knew all about that. Although sometimes he even thought it would have been easier if his dad had died instead of just taken off. The sadness might be easier to deal with, because it wouldn't be so wrapped up in anger, too.

And if he was being honest with himself, there was another reason Nick wanted to pull this delivery off. Ever since his dad had left, he had wanted to do something really big—something that would show he had stick-to-itiveness, unlike his dad. At the same time, he wanted to do something that would make his dad proud —or at least show him that Nick would be okay without him—even though he wouldn't actually be around to see it. The mix of conflicting emotions was very strange. He tried not to think about it too much.

But he couldn't explain all of that to Burger. Could hardly explain it to himself. "Look, we only have to be dead for a few minutes, okay? We'll help each other out, watch each other. And when we take off the costumes, we'll be back to normal, just like before."

Burger grinned. "We weren't exactly normal before."

"You know what I mean."

"All right, man. I'll stay dead for you." Burger shrugged. "This has been the weirdest day ever."

"I'd definitely put it in my top five." Nick jerked his head toward the road. "Let's go get that truck."

17

THE U-HAUL RENTAL CENTER WAS ONLY A COUPLE of blocks away, within easy floating distance.

They pushed their ghostly bodies right through the locked chain-link fence (Burger said it tickled), then through the door to the front lobby, and finally into the locked office where the keys to the trucks were kept.

"Wait. Isn't this, like, stealing?" Burger said.

"Not at all. First, we're going to bring the truck back. Second, we'll just put the rental fee in the mail. As soon as we get our share of the money." Nick scanned the keys, trying to figure out how they were organized. He wanted to make sure to get the biggest truck they had.

"So why didn't you just bring some cash tonight?"

Nick shot Burger a look, raising one bluish-white eyebrow. "Ghosts don't have pockets."

"Oh. Right."

Nick ran his shimmering finger along a row of keys. Burger set his feet and placed his palms together like he was on a swimming-pool diving board, then dove into the air and floated through the walls of the office and out of sight. Nick continued to scan the keys until he found one for a twenty-foot model.

When he returned to the lobby, he found Burger standing in front of a mirror, holding a stapler in one shimmering hand and a coffee cup in the other. He was slowly waving them back and forth.

"What are you doing?" Nick said. "Wait—never mind. I don't want to know."

"Here, take a look."

Nick glanced at the mirror. Because there was no reflection of Burger's ghostly form, it looked like the objects were floating around in midair all by themselves.

"Isn't it spoo-o-o-o-o-ky?" Burger made his voice waver dramatically.

"Not really. Let's go."

"Come on. That's only because you know that it's me. What if we snuck into someone's house and did this? Do you know how funny that would be? Chet would be so scared he'd pee somebody *else's* pants."

Nick sighed. "Can we just go? I told you, we have a job to do."

Burger plunked the stapler and coffee cup back on the desk and scoffed. "Mrs. Monahan was right. Living is wasted on people like you."

"Seriously, Burger? Mrs. Monahan is *dead*. She's probably not the best role model."

"But just think about it!" Burger floated up to the ceiling and then pushed off with both hands, doing a backstroke swimming motion as he glided around the room. "No homework. No tests. No chores. Just total freedom." Burger air-swam right through the walls and out of the lobby.

"I thought you were the one who didn't want to be dead in the first place."

"I'm getting used to it. It's okay to have a little fun, you know."

The scary part was that Burger was actually starting to make some sense. Being a ghost did have its advantages. Total weightlessness. Was this what the astronauts felt like in the zero gravity of space? Nick had to admit, it was quite a rush.

And it was more than just the weightlessness of his body. As soon as Nick put the costume on, his worries and stress had disappeared along with his body parts. He had to concentrate harder and harder just to keep his mind focused on the task at hand. It would be so much more fun to just float around and not be bothered about anything.

He realized that Burger pretty much lived his life like that, anyway. Burger was going to make a great dead person someday.

And really, was it so bad? When Nick thought about taking the costume off, his mind started to go as fuzzy as the outline of his ghostly body. What could it hurt to stay in the afterlife for a while? Maybe a few days. Or a week. It would be like a vacation from himself. No more hustling every day at school, no more worrying about how much money was in the TIPS can when the rent was due at the end of the month, no more—

"Someone's coming!" Burger zoomed through the wall and crashed into Nick. Sort of. Since they were both ghosts, he actually just kind of softly nudged up against him.

The handle to the door jiggled and they could hear the scraping of a key in the lock from the other side.

"We have to hide!" Burger whispered.

"No, we don't. We're ghosts. Just stand still."

"Oh. Yeah."

The door opened and a big guy in a security-guard outfit walked in and frowned at the open key case. He approached and flicked on a flashlight, tracing the beam over the rows of keys.

"What if he finds one missing?" Burger whispered.

Nick started to hold a finger over his bluish-white lips, but it was too late. The guard spun around and swept his flashlight across the room.

Nick stood still and started to hold his breath . . . when he realized that he hadn't been breathing in the first place. Couldn't remember the last time he had taken a breath. Man, these costumes were good.

The guard's shoulders shivered all over for a minute, then he turned, swung the key-case door shut, and hurried away.

Before he could get out the door, Burger zipped over and flicked the back of the guard's hat, which flipped off his head and tumbled to the floor.

"GET. OUT." Burger used a deep voice. "GO. HOME."

The guard stood frozen to the spot, eyes wide and hands shaking.

For good measure, Burger grabbed the stapler and coffee cup and waved them around again.

That did it. The guard grabbed his hat and flew out the door, slamming it behind him. They could hear pounding footsteps growing fainter and more doors slamming.

Burger raised up the stapler and cup triumphantly, a big ghost grin on his face. "See? I told you it would work!"

"You're going to get us caught. Why not just let him leave on his own?"

Burger set the objects down and looked at Nick. "Seriously? You're supposed to be the one with the brains. How are we supposed to borrow a truck with him sniffing around? That guy's going home and won't be back for the rest of the night. Guaranteed."

"Oh." Nick had to admit, it was actually a pretty good plan. "I guess being semidead has improved your brain."

"Told ya. I'll never wanna take this thing off." Burger floated up to the ceiling and started his air-swimming again.

Nick had an overwhelming urge to toss the keys aside and float around with Burger, to stop trying so hard.

But he knew that it was the weird influence of the costumes that was making him feel like this. He tried to fight it off, to think more like himself again. It helped to envision Connor Flanagan, very much alive, and scared, and keeping up his vigil in the middle of the forest. Nick had made a deal, given the guy his word. That had to mean something. Time to snap Burger out of it.

"Hot dogs. Kettle corn. Gravy. Root-beer floats. Hash browns. Steak and—"

Burger stopped and looked at him. "What are you doing?"

"Ghosts don't need food. If you keep that costume on, you'll never do your favorite thing in the world again."

"No eating?" Burger dropped back down to the floor. "Let's get that truck and get out of here."

Nick was in the driver's seat as the U-Haul eased out of the rental-center parking lot. His mom usually let him drive the last half mile to their house, because the road was always deserted, so he was comfortable behind the wheel. Burger was the lookout. He kept his head on a swivel, scanning the surrounding streets.

"What if someone spots a truck driving around with no one in the front seat?"

"It's almost three in the morning. I think we'll be able to avoid the one or two cars that might be out."

"But we should be prepared. What if a cop pulls us over? You don't even have a license."

"A license?" Nick scoffed. "It's not going to come to that. We just pull over, float away, and go get another truck. The cop won't be able to see us."

Burger settled into his seat and smiled. "Man, I'm going to miss being a ghost."

"Don't worry. You'll be dead someday."

Burger leaned back and put his bluish-white hands behind his head. "It must be comforting for you. Knowing exactly how you're going to die."

"What's that supposed to mean?" Nick said. "How am I going to die?"

"My guess is that it happens about two minutes after Chet finds out you're in love with his sister."

"I'm not in love with anybody." Nick took a swing at Burger, but his hand passed right through his friend's body. Burger just chuckled.

Nick drove down the quiet back roads of Bayside, trying to stay away from streetlights. He made sure to drive exactly the speed limit.

As he steered the truck past the city line and toward

Chuckanut Drive, it was undeniable that he was getting weaker. The longer he kept the costume on, the harder it was to turn the steering wheel or pump the break. Was he fading away, like a real ghost? Nick got the feeling that his heart would have sped up with fear if it had been beating in the first place. He nudged the speedometer upward, determined to make it home before he lost his grip on the material world altogether.

He wondered if the same thing was happening to Burger. His friend had been quiet for a long time, and Nick had been so focused on the road that he hadn't even looked over at him. He turned to ask Burger if he was—

"Aaaaaagh!"

Ghost-Burger was back to being just Burger. He was curled up in the passenger seat with his head resting against the window. He was snoring. And he was naked.

When Nick yelled, Burger's eyes flew open. "What?" He stared at the steering wheel. "Nick! Where are you? NICK?"

"You're ... you're ..."

Burger looked down at his body. "Aaaaaaagh!"

He folded in on himself, trying to cover up. The flimsy material of the ghost costume slipped off and dropped to the floorboards. Burger snatched it back up and threw it over his head. Nothing. He just looked like a naked kid barely covered in Saran Wrap.

"It doesn't work anymore," Nick said. "Don't you remember the second time you tried the gorilla costume?"

"Where are my clothes?"

"Oh, no. We left them back at the—"

"Watch the road!"

Nick suddenly realized they were drifting toward the ditch. He tried to swerve away, but his strength had faded even further. It wasn't enough. Burger had to lunge over, grab the steering wheel, and spin it. The truck's tires dug into the soft shoulder, the whole thing leaned sickeningly toward the ditch for a few moments, on the verge of tipping over... then careened back onto the road.

Burger collapsed back into his seat and exhaled. "That was close." He looked over at the driver's seat. "It's really weird not to be able to see you."

"Well, it's even weirder for me to be able to see you." Nick stared straight ahead through the windshield. "You're still naked."

"Oh. Yeah." Burger rummaged around behind his seat and pulled out a tarp used to cover furniture in the back of the U-Haul. He draped it over himself.

The boys were quiet for a while, searching the road for any sign of people or approaching cars.

"I wonder why my costume stopped working and yours didn't."

"I don't know. Maybe because you fell asleep?" Nick looked down at himself. "Man, I hope that's it. I don't want this thing to stop working until we get this truck safely home."

Burger picked up the flimsy sheet of material and

studied it. "I wish these things came with an instruction manual."

"No kidding."

"Your voice sounds quieter. Like it's coming from farther away."

Nick felt a rising panic and tightened his grip on the steering wheel. "We better get this thing parked pretty quick."

It took another half hour to get to their destination. Nick maneuvered the U-Haul onto one of the weed-choked old logging roads close to Burger's house and situated it behind a thicket of bushes. They'd be back for it first thing after spending the night at Burger's, so he wasn't too worried about anybody finding it.

"We need to go to your house and try to get some sleep," Nick said. "We have a lot of work to do in the morning."

"I wish I was a ghost again." Burger sighed and pulled the tarp around himself before he eased his door open and stepped out into the night. "Ghosts don't get cold."

Nick disagreed. He couldn't wait to get this thing off. Better to be cold—or lonely or heartbroken or whatever —than to be just numb and weightless. Better to have at least the chance to experience the good, even if it was sometimes mixed up with the bad. For the first time in a while, he was really looking forward to being himself.

CONNOR FLANAGAN WAS TOO DEEP IN THE FOREST to see the sunrise. He became aware of the new day when a dull, gray light slowly revealed the fog that was creeping between the trees surrounding the delivery truck.

It was so cold that sleep had been impossible. All night he'd been tempted to throw the costumes into a big heap and crawl into the middle of them for warmth. But he hadn't dared. With his luck he'd have tossed and turned as he slept, accidentally slipped his arms and legs into different costumes, and then woken up as a vampire-giraffe-zombie covered in feathers and tentacles.

He rubbed his hands together and blew on them. Man, he hoped those kids got back soon. They needed to—

Rrrrrring!

He jumped up so fast he cracked his head on the ceiling.

Rrrrrring! Rrrrrring!

Connor crawled through the back of the overturned truck, looking for the crystal-ball phone.

He pushed a stack of garment boxes aside and was confronted by Mary Goodwin's face again. It appeared to be floating, neckless, suspended in crystal-ball juice like a biology lab specimen.

She scowled at Connor until he picked up the receiver.

"Humph! Least you took off the bear costume. Don't ever mess with the merchandise again, boy." She smacked her lips together wetly. "Why'd you go and slip that on, anyway?"

"I don't... that is, I didn't try to... I mean, it wasn't—"

"Oh, hush your fuss. Just see that it never happens again. Now, today's the day, so tell me what I need to hear—you all set to make this delivery in a timely manner?"

"Well... I actually wanted to talk to you about that." Connor rubbed the back of his neck nervously. "These costumes. They seem, you know, pretty dangerous. I'm not sure it's, um, exactly a good idea to let people put them on and—"

"Nonsense. These rich fools need some way to spend all that money, and they pay top dollar for specialty items."

"But what if—"

"Look, boy, they'll throw these on and chase each other around for a few hours, but then the costumes stop working at midnight on Halloween. Permanently. Same thing if they take 'em off. Or if they fall asleep. That's usually what older folk do, you realize? Have too much to drink and fall asleep and let life pass 'em by. You think I'd let my magical creations loose in the world for good? No, sir. No profit in that. After tonight, those are just dime-store costumes. That's why it's so important you get the delivery made on time."

"I just think that—"

"Well, I don't pay your family to think, do I?" As her voice rose in anger, that skin of hers started to wrinkle and droop again and slough down her cheeks. In those moments, Connor could see the terrible mark that all of those years had made, not just on her face, but also on something deeper inside her.

Mary Goodwin pushed and prodded her skin back into place, until she looked young again. "Now tell me true, can you make that delivery on time, or not?"

Connor nodded. "Yes, I should be able to." He took a deep breath. "There was a little trouble with the truck, but it's getting sorted out. As soon as they get back, I can finally—"

"THEY?"

The shriek was so loud that Connor dropped the receiver and got tangled in the twisty black cord. Mary Goodwin's flesh instantly wrinkled and sagged so much that Connor thought it might melt right off of her head and just leave a skull leering at him. Connor didn't think he'd be able to handle that.

She pushed her face against the inside of the crystal ball, her features stretching and distorting in that fish-eye lens way.

"WHAT DO YOU MEAN, THEY???"

Oh, no. "It's not what you think." He fumbled with the cord, shouting so that she could still hear him. "They don't know anything about... that is to say, they're just getting a replacement truck for—"

Mary Goodwin thrust her face forward until the entire crystal ball was filled with nothing but a pale, watery eyeball. "You don't get to take on partners! This has been a solo job for over three centuries. I swear, not even your great-great-great-great-grandpa Jedidiah was this pathetic, and he was no more'n a half-wit with nothing but a little mule-and-buggy rig for deliveries."

She pulled back so Connor could see all of her again, and she didn't bother to pretty herself up this time.

"I'm sorry. So, so sorry." Connor finally untangled the cord and held the receiver back up to this mouth. "But I had to. There was no other way. And besides, they're just kids. They won't—"

"KIDS?!?" Globs of spit flew out of her mouth and splattered the inside of the crystal ball. "Kids is the worst. Too stupid to be afraid. And what's more, they believe purty near anything. And everything. Minds haven't been shut

down by life, like the older kind." She shook her head in disgust, the soft skin jiggling all over. "You can't let kids anywhere near those costumes, you hear? Grown folks get a little thrill outta the costumes, just sorta flirtin' with the magic, you see. They only get a taste. But kids? No telling what can happen if a dirty kid gets his hands on one."

Mary Goodwin stopped to catch her breath, squishy flesh turning red with the exertion of yelling. Connor seized his chance to wrap up the conversation.

"It'll be okay, I promise. They're just bringing me a new truck, then—"

"A new truck? Boy, you must be even slower than I thought. Maybe you noticed that there's something special about the truck your dad left you? That not every truck can go through the wormholes?"

"It's okay. Really. We're close to the drop-off location. As soon as I finish up the delivery, I can get Dad's truck back on the road and come right back. I'll take care of everything."

"Oh, you best take care of those kids, right enough." She raised her hand, which was gripping that big hunting knife again. "After these *kids* bring you that truck, you just make sure they're in no shape to be telling any tales. You hear me?" She slowly drew the blade across the sagging flesh of her throat to make her point. Then she let her tongue loll out of the side of her mouth and made strangled, gaspy death-rattle noises for good measure.

"Oh! No, I couldn't do anything like that. I'll have to make them understand that—"

"If you can't take care of your business, then I sure as heckfire will." Mary Goodwin stepped back farther and Connor could see her entire body, which seemed to be withering and stooping inside her rough, brown robe the longer she stayed angry.

And worse, standing behind her were three of the huge, misshapen mud-creatures that had loaded up the delivery truck back home.

She stuck a gnarled finger out of her sleeve and jabbed it at Connor. "If you don't put those kids down, then the same fate awaits every living Flanagan. I own your entire family, boy. Always have, always will. Isn't that right, boys?" She turned to look at the mud-creatures. They lifted their heads, stretched open mouths that dribbled out pebbles and bits of rotting leaves, and started up a chorus of inhuman moaning. They reached toward him with grasping fingers made of decayed earth.

Connor shivered all over. He shoved the crystal ball back into the corner and stacked a couple of boxes on top of it. Then he found a tarp and draped it over the whole pile for good measure. He simply wasn't able to think about Mary Goodwin anymore. He could only take this day one impossible, terrifying thing at a time.

Cold, miserable, and scared, he drew his knees up to his chest and wrapped his arms around them, huddling into himself for warmth.

Connor drifted into a fitful sleep. His brain filled with half memories/half dreams of witches and wormholes and magical curses. So when he first heard the voices and the snapping branches, he thought for one wild second that the mud-creatures had found him and were stomping right to the truck to finish him off. He scrambled out the back and dove behind a thicket of bushes.

But as his heartbeat calmed down, he realized that those were human voices. Speaking actual words. Not the gravelly moaning from the crystal ball.

Finally! Those boys had come back. Time to get this delivery finished and be done with it. And maybe just having a task—the mindless, physical chore of hauling the costumes up the trail and loading them into the U-Haul at the road above—would help take his mind off his terror. He shook his sleep-stiffened arms and legs, then tried to rub the soreness out. If he could just—

Wait. There were too many voices. Did those kids tell their friends?

He peeked out from around the bush and looked up the trail, but it was lost in fog.

One of the voices rose suddenly and was followed by a chorus of laughter. Definitely too many people. Sounded like eight or nine.

Not good.

The thing that emerged from the fog looked like a cross between a wheelchair, an ATV, and some sort of moon rover from a sci-fi movie. The guy up on top surveyed the clearing like a king from his throne.

"Oh, yes. I think we found it, fellas."

Behind him, over half a dozen burly teenagers stepped out from between the trees. They stopped and studied the truck.

"I knew it," the biggest one said. "As soon as Hector put on that gorilla suit and completely lost it, I knew those stupid kids were hiding something down here."

Connor Flanagan couldn't breathe. It felt like his heart was being squeezed by a vise.

A few of the guys stepped toward the truck, but the guy in the robo-wheelchair said, "Stop," and they obeyed right away.

"That was some seriously weird stuff back in town. We need to do this right." He steered his way in between the crowd of guys and the overturned truck. Then he spun the chair around to face the troops. "Ox, Mitchell, and Weinheimer: take the left flank. The rest of you, approach from the other side. Slowly." He reached behind his back and withdrew a machete with a metallic hiss. "If there's anything crazy in there, we'll be ready."

Carefully, the mob advanced on the truck.

Connor's body reacted on its own, fueled by panic. Crouching, keeping the truck between him and the group of guys, he dashed forward and lunged his head and shoulders into the open doors of the cargo bay.

He latched on to the first garment box his hands found and then scampered back behind the bushes.

Connor glanced into the clearing. They hadn't seen him. The guys fanned out in a semicircle. All had shoulders hunched, hands out, knees bent. Athletic stances. Ready for a fight.

Connor studied the box. As nervous as he was to climb into another costume, he knew it was his only chance to save the rest of the cargo. No way would these guys stick around if a bear burst out of the forest. Or something even worse.

"Ox," called the guy on wheels, "work your way around to the back, look through those doors. Let us know what you find."

"Got it."

Connor swallowed drily. This was it.

Holding his breath, he eased the top off the box to reveal the contents. It wasn't grizzly fur. Instead, he found shimmering green scales.

Connor unfurled the costume from the box and it unraveled in yards and yards of material. It was huge. An alligator?

That might do the trick.

He lifted the head to put it on and found that it featured oversize cat's eyes, long snout, curved fangs, and long, pointy ears. Not an alligator.

A dragon.

That should *definitely* do the trick.

18

BURGER HELD UP THE COAT, EXAMINING IT. "THESE
clothes smell weird."

"My dad left them. Haven't been out of these bags in
over two years."

"Oh. Sorry, dude."

"Don't worry about it." Nick tried to find a way to set
the fedora on his head so that it wouldn't fall down into
his eyes. Then he buttoned up the tan overcoat. The boys
were going to have to drive the U-Haul in broad daylight,
and Nick wanted to look older in case they were spotted.
He thought it could work. From a distance.

He rolled up the sleeves of the coat, freeing his hands
for driving, then looked at himself in the side mirror,
trying to remember the last time he had seen his dad

wearing the same outfit. Nick wished these clothes could work like the costumes, and magically turn him into his dad. Or at least let Nick think like him for a little while. Maybe then he could understand why his dad had left.

But it wasn't like that. He was just wearing a too-big coat and an old hat. "Come on," Nick said. "Let's get to work." He and Burger climbed into the cab of the U-Haul, eased it out from behind the bushes, and drove between the trees.

When they turned onto the main road, traffic was light, but they still encountered the occasional car. Nick tilted his head away from the passing drivers, shielding his face with the brim of the hat as much as he could, but it didn't matter. As far as he could tell, no one looked twice. Grown-ups never seemed to notice much of anything other than what they were doing.

The midafternoon sun was trying to peek out from behind all the clouds. The boys had slept late after their all-night adventure, and then eaten a big lunch. They needed energy for the work ahead of them. Thinking about it, Nick started to feel jittery. He bounced a little in his seat.

"You nervous?" Burger said.

"I'm just trying to concentrate on what it will be like when we're all done. The money." Nick kept even pressure on the gas pedal and steered carefully. "That helps. How about you?"

"Maybe a little. But this has totally been worth it. I

always wanted something cool to happen around here, you know?" Burger leaned back in the seat, put his shoes up on the glove box.

Closer to town, traffic started to pick up a little. "Put your feet down; you look like a kid."

"Whatever you say, boss. I'm just trying to—"

"Oh, crap!" Nick rounded a corner and hit the brakes, too hard, throwing the boys forward against their seat belts.

"What?" Burger picked up his hat, which had tumbled onto the dashboard.

"Look!"

Down the road, three police cars sat lengthwise, end to end, creating a roadblock. Red and blue lights flashed on top. A stream of cars was stopped in the middle of the street.

"Do you think they're looking for us?"

"What?" Burger said. "Why?"

"I don't know, maybe the U-Haul people opened up shop this morning, reported a missing vehicle?" Nick scanned the road, looking for a way to do a U-turn, but cars were already piling up behind them, and the truck was just too big to maneuver. "So the cops set up a road-block, don't let anyone leave town until they find it."

"What do we do?"

Nick considered. They could just abandon the truck and make a dash for it. Work their way among the trees for cover. As long as they didn't get run down right away and caught red-handed, they should be fine—there was nothing to link them to the truck.

"Look—there's the KPUG van. Turn on the radio."

Nick pressed POWER and tuned in to 1170 AM.

"—should stay indoors until the wild animal is apprehended. Police say it's acting very erratically and should in no way be approached."

"Is anyone saying where he might have come from, Janet?"

"There are no indications at this time. The nearest zoo is in Abbotsford, British Columbia, but that's over thirty miles away. This big fella would've had to hitchhike to come all the way to Bayside."

"Ha-ha. Well, keep us posted, Janet."

Nick and Burger looked at each other. "What the—"

RO—AAH—OAGGHH!

A snarling, slavering gorilla burst from the cover of trees at the side of the road. The people who had been standing beside their cars, waiting for the roadblock to clear, dove back in and slammed the doors shut behind them. Nick could hear their muffled shouts as the huge ape ran right in between the cars.

Nick white-knuckled the steering wheel and Burger gasped.

The shock and terror of seeing a wild beast around all

of those people distracted them a few moments before they were able to piece together what had happened.

"Dude." Burger breathed heavily, watching through the windshield with wide eyes. "That gorilla looks very familiar."

"Tell me about it."

When the police officers drew their guns, the ape dove behind a Volvo station wagon and crouched down behind it, shielding himself. Staying low, he worked his way toward the driver's door, splayed feet shuffling along on the asphalt. The officers fanned out and tried to flank him.

An Animal Control van screeched to a halt on the other side of the roadblock and three guys in white suits jumped out. Two of them were holding a net stretched between them while the third held a long-barreled tranquilizer gun at the ready.

The hunched-over gorilla reached out with an enormous black hand and tugged on the door handle of the Volvo. It was locked.

The circle of police and Animal Control workers expanded to encompass the line of parked cars. One of the cops produced a megaphone. "APPROACH WITH CAUTION. MAKE SURE NO PEOPLE ARE IN YOUR LINE OF FIRE."

Nick scrunched down in his seat until just his eyes peeped up above the dashboard.

The gorilla banged on the station wagon's driver's-side door. Someone inside screamed.

The cops motioned for people in their cars to get down. The Animal Control guys looped around, getting a clear line of sight on the beast, and lifted the net higher.

The gorilla looked back at them, then let loose with another roar and smashed a furry fist into the Volvo's window. It shattered, bits of glass bouncing off the road. The gorilla reached inside the car, popped the lock, and yanked the door open.

The driver, a middle-aged lady, tried to get away, but she was stopped by her seat belt and too panicked to realize it was keeping her leashed to the car. She struggled wildly, arms and legs flailing, until the gorilla reached into the vehicle with a thickly muscled arm. Then she stopped screaming and got very, very still, her eyes wide with terror.

The ape leaned forward while the woman stayed stock-still, staring at him without blinking. An instant later, the lady's seat belt fell off of her. Then the gorilla turned his body so she would have room to exit the car and he stretched out his arm in a polite *after-you* gesture.

The woman remained frozen, staring at the gorilla. Her face was only inches from his black fur and mouth full of oversize teeth.

"NO SUDDEN MOVEMENTS, MA'AM, BUT STEP AWAY FROM THE CAR. SLOW–LY," the cop with the megaphone said.

The woman eased herself out of the driver's seat, never taking her eyes off the gorilla. After she made it a few shaky steps from the vehicle, she burst into a run and collapsed into the arms of a police officer, sobbing.

The Animal Control guys lunged forward and threw the net, but it was too late. The gorilla jumped into the car and slammed the door; the net clanged harmlessly against the side.

An instant later, the Volvo's engine roared to life. The tires spun against the wet asphalt until a wisp of smoke rose up behind the car, then squealed as the Volvo took off. The gorilla, crammed into the seat and hunched over with his head scraping the ceiling of the cab, spun the little wheel in his huge grip, and rocketed away in the opposite direction.

The cops holstered their guns, jumped in their cars, and took off in pursuit, sirens screaming. The Animal Control van followed close behind.

Inside the truck, the boys exhaled heavily. "Well, the good news is that I don't think anyone's going to notice a couple of kids in a stolen U-Haul," Burger said.

"We've got way bigger problems than that now. They must've tried on your gorilla costume. Chet and his friends."

"I know. And it worked this time. Why did it work again?"

Nick shook his head, trying to clear it so he could think again. "Who knows? Maybe because it was somebody different? Not you again, I mean."

"I'm telling you, we need instruction manuals!"

They stared out the window. Everyone had stepped back out of their cars and was yelling into cell phones. A TV truck pulled up next to the radio van, and an instant later they both took off in the direction of the police chase.

"Okay. We have to think." Nick took a deep breath. "If those high schoolers figured out how the costumes work, then they'd go back to the trail. That's where they found you with the costume. And they know we keep stuff stashed down there." He started up the engine on the U-Haul again. "We have to get back to the delivery truck. Now."

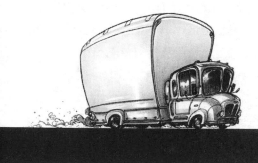

19

THE BOYS RAN DOWN THE HIDDEN TRAIL AND
into the clearing with the overturned delivery truck.
Burger raced ahead and reached the open cargo bay first.
"Oh, no!"

"What?"

"The costumes. They're gone!"

Nick caught up and saw it was true. There were a few
scattered boxes lying around, but the storage area was
nearly empty. Both boys just stood and stared.

"Oh, man. If all of those guys put costumes on..."
They could both picture it: a horde of real-life monsters
unleashed on Bayside—on the one night of the year when
little kids were encouraged to walk around after dark.

If Nick and Burger had nearly lost control during their

backyard brawl, what would Chet and Ox and the rest of them be like inside those things?

Nick paced back and forth across the clearing. "Okay, let's stay calm. Assess the situation. We don't even know for sure that it was them," he said. "Maybe Connor took the costumes during the night and stashed them somewhere. For safekeeping. I don't see him anywhere, so there's a chance that he could've—"

A low, rumbling growl filled the clearing, the bass so deep that Nick could feel it in his chest. The boys dove into the back of the truck for cover and huddled on the floor.

"That didn't sound like a bear," Burger whispered. "That sounded bigger."

They crept to the lip of the cargo bay and peered out. A clump of bushes at the edge of the clearing started shaking all over.

The green, reptilian head that pushed through the leaves was so big that it dominated Nick's field of vision as if it was in IMAX 3-D. It smoothly wove back and forth through the thicket of bushes in that glide-y way that only snakes can move.

"That's a dragon," Burger whispered.

"I know what it is. I've been to the movies."

"But...but...but that's *really* a dragon."

Nick understood why Burger was freaked out. Not just that the thing was so huge. It was more that its scaly, slithery, serpentine *dragon-ness* seemed totally out of the place in the middle of their familiar woods.

The boys pressed themselves as flat as possible to the floor.

"What if it's Chet or one of his friends? We're toast."

"Shhh. I think maybe it's hurt." Nick pointed.

As the dragon's body entered the clearing, it became evident there was something wrong. It was crawling, not walking. The great beast pulled itself along on scaly fore-legs, belly scraping along the forest floor, then stopped. It breathed heavily, steam rising from that long snout. Then its front claws reached out and dragged its giant snakelike torso forward another ten feet or so, before it stopped again. Thick ropes of drool splattered to the ground as it panted.

When the second half of its elongated body emerged from the forest, it looked deflated. Flattened. No muscles or bones, just droopy, scaly flesh that pooled in folds on the ground. The hind legs dragged lifelessly behind. It seemed to be taking a lot of energy for the dragon to lug the inert half of its body out from the trees.

"Look at its back legs," Nick whispered. "Is that... do you think that's what happens when Chet gets in a cos-tume? The legs still don't work?"

The dragon's head suddenly swung around to face the truck. The boys held their breath.

Bowling-ball-size nostrils contracted as the massive

reptile sniffed the air. Then it slither-limped toward the open cargo bay, dragging its scaly belly through mud and clumps of pine needles.

"Dude. Maybe we shouldn't have hidden in the one place where we can't run away."

"Do you think that's Chet, or what?"

"How am I supposed to know? It's not like these costumes come with name tags."

Nick scanned the storage area for something—anything—that he might be able to use in a fight. Didn't fantasy heroes try to stab big monsters in the eye?

The dragon's head loomed closer, completely filling the doorway. A yellow eyeball, bigger than a pumpkin and with catlike irises, thrust closer and peered into the back of the truck. When the dragon spotted the boys, its rumbling growls rose higher in pitch.

"That sounds weird. Do you think maybe it's whimpering?"

"Or else that's the noise it makes right before it blows fire everywhere."

The dragon stretched out one enormous paw toward the truck, talons as thick as broadswords. But with its hind legs withered and lifeless, it couldn't support itself on only one leg. The dragon lost its balance and face-planted in the soft earth.

The dragon lifted its neck at an awkward angle, spitting out leaves and licking mud off of its fangs. Then it

shook his head, did some more of that whimpering...
and turned to bonk his head against a nearby tree in
frustration.

The boys looked at each other. "That's gotta be Connor,"
they both said at the same time.

The dragon wearily swung his head around and bonked it against the side of the truck, but it was so massive
that the wall caved in and the entire truck was pushed
several feet across the clearing.

"Whoa!" The boys scrambled to their feet and jumped
out the back.

They stood in front of the dragon. Its mouth was so
big that Burger could have stepped right inside without
ducking.

"Connor... is that you?"

The dragon tilted its head and studied the boys, then
glanced back at its twisting torso, and slowly nodded
once.

"He doesn't seem too sure," Burger said.

"You know how it is inside those things. We have to
get him out of there. Quick."

Burger took a few cautious steps forward. "Okay, show
me your neck, big guy. Let me find that zipper."

The dragon tilted his head curiously again, looked
back and forth between both boys, then slowly, uncer-
tainly, tipped it up, exposing his neck.

But when Burger got closer, those massive nostrils

contracted again and the dragon dropped his head and snorted. A jet of orange flame shot out and blasted right over Burger, just missing his flyaway mop of whitish-blond hair.

The dragon snapped its jaws as Burger scrambled away. Then the beast lunged forward and swung its claws, slamming its enormous paw into a tree trunk. The tree splintered in half under the force of the mighty blow. A shower of pine needles fell down on the boys like confetti.

Burger slipped in the mud. Nick rushed forward, grabbed his friend, and tried to pull him away, but he couldn't get his footing in the muck.

The dragon lurched toward the boys, but it was brought up short by his lifeless hindquarters. As the beast was trying to drag itself away, the top half of the tree trunk slowly fell and smashed down right on top of its tail. The beast howled in pain, lost its balance, and face-planted in the mud again.

It was a very clumsy dragon.

When it started to collect itself to rise again, Nick saw a piece of metal glinting on the scaly throat. As the dragon snorted steam, Nick dashed forward, grabbed the end of the zipper, and yanked for all he was worth.

Connor stumbled out of the dragon's neck, dripping with sweat and steaming in the cool autumn air, while the costume slumped lifelessly to the ground.

"Dude. You tried to barbecue us."

"Serves you right!" The costume might have been off, but Connor was still in a rage. "The costumes are gone! A group of guys just showed up and took them. *All* of them." He pointed at the boys. "And it's your fault, isn't it? Those are the guys you were telling me about."

He lunged toward Nick, but his legs were shaky and his knees buckled.

Nick backed away, his hands held out in front of him. "We're sorry. Really. We'll help you figure out how—"

"We have to get them back!" The anger in Connor's eyes was gone, clouded over with fear now. "Have to get them back...right now...she's going to ruin us, all of us...." He looked up at the boys again as if seeing them for the first time. "Go home—hide!—don't tell anyone... I'm sorry...so sorry that I dragged you into—"

"Whoa, whoa. Take it easy."

Connor held his head in his hands. Burger picked him up out of the mud, led him over to the fallen tree, and sat him down.

"I'm so sorry. About the fire and the claws and everything," Connor said, staring at the ground. "I never meant to hurt you. Something happens to me when I'm in those costumes."

Nick and Burger shot each other a look. "So you feel it, too?"

"Yeah. I never get that mad." He glanced up, a sheepish

expression on his face. "Plus, I'm not going to lie, you two smelled delicious. And even though part of me knew it was wrong to eat you...most of me didn't care."

Nick glanced at the empty cargo bay. "No time to worry about that right now. Tell us everything that happened."

Connor let out a shaky breath. "There was this group of guys. Teenagers. The leader was riding in some sort of ATV-wheelchair thing. They cleared out the whole truck."

"Is that why you put the costume on?"

Connor nodded. "But I couldn't stop them. You saw me. I wasn't a very good dragon. Couldn't even move half of it."

Burger threw up his hands in frustration. "Man, that creepy lady really should've given you some instruction manuals."

"Tell me about it." Connor put his head in his hands again. "I ended up just hiding in the forest the whole time until I heard you two."

Nick got up and walked along the length of the dragon costume, examining it. Just before the tail disappeared under the fallen tree, he found what he was looking for.

"Burger, look at this." He grabbed a fistful of the material and held it up.

"Is that another zipper?"

"Yeah. I think this must be so big that it's a two-man costume. No wonder Connor couldn't move the back half."

Burger shook his head. "Instruction manuals," he muttered.

Nick walked back and sat down next to Connor on the log. "We need to figure out what we're going to do. Now."

"I found out that the costumes stop working at midnight," Connor said. "That's good news, right?"

"What a rip-off!" Burger said. Connor and Nick stared at him. "What? Okay, I know those things are a little messed up, but I wanted a chance to get in one again. Come on, they're fun."

"We're past the fun stage, Burger. People are in danger. Those guys will be able to do some serious damage before midnight." Nick fixed Burger with a stare. "And you realize where they're headed, right?"

Burger's eyes got wide. "The party," he breathed.

"That's it!" Connor said. "They said something about a Halloween party. You mean you guys actually know where it is?"

"We were planning on heading over there tonight," Burger said. "A ton of kids from our grade are going to be there."

Nick shook his head slowly. "That would not be a good place for a group of monsters to do a lot of damage."

20

NICK COULDN'T STOP PACING BACK AND FORTH.
The brainstorming session was not going well, and as the
light in the woods started to grow dimmer, it became clear
they were running out of time.

Connor jumped off the log and started for the trail.
"We need to get going."

"But we need a plan first," Nick said.

"I have a plan." Connor stopped halfway across the
clearing and turned to face the boys. "I'm calling the
police."

"No, you can't—"

"And the fire department. And the mayor, and the
city council, and the National Guard, and anyone else
who will answer. This entire town needs some major

protection until midnight. It doesn't matter anymore about what happens afterward."

"Okay, I know it's a risk, but what about this?" Nick marched over to the dragon costume. "Look, it even has wings." He held up the folds of scarlet material fastened to the back. "Now that we know it's a two-man costume, Burger and I can both get right in there, fly over to Hayley's house, and take the costumes back. Even if those guys have already put them on, they're not going to be any match for a dragon."

"No way," Burger said.

"Why?"

"I am *not* going to turn myself into a dragon butt. Just not happening."

Connor stepped in between them. "No one should get into that costume, under any circumstances." He looked at the scaly material with haunted eyes. "It was different than the bear," he said quietly.

"What do you mean?"

"In the bear, my thoughts were...I don't know, *bear-ish*, I guess. Normal, animal-type stuff. But in the dragon..." Connor paused and shuddered. "It was darker. Murkier. The only thing I could think about was how hungry I was. Nothing else mattered. And I mean nothing." He looked up at the boys. "You saw me—I almost ate the big kid here."

Nick dropped the wing material to the forest floor and threw his hands up in exasperation. "But using the costumes is the only thing that gives us a chance against all of those guys."

"Wait," said Burger. "Has anyone even checked to see if Chet left any other costumes behind?"

Within seconds, the three were inside the cargo bay, searching through a jumble of garment boxes. They were all empty. Burger finally reached a tarp in the very back of the truck.

"Hey, I think I found something!"

He jumped back out, holding two boxes and what looked like a crystal ball attached to an old-timey phone receiver. He hefted the boxes in one hand. "Feels like there's still something in here!" Then he nodded to the crystal ball. "And what's this?"

"Never mind," Connor said. He grabbed the orb and wrapped it back up in the tarp.

Nick took one of the boxes from Burger and shook it. "You're right. Definitely something in here."

"I hope it's awesome," Burger said. "We're going to need something good to go up against those guys."

Nick took a deep breath and pulled the top off his box. Inside lay a folded piece of plain, brown fabric.

"Is that it?" Burger said.

Nick unfurled the costume. Just a simple brown robe with a hood. "Is it a . . . what, a monk? That doesn't seem very helpful."

"Hey, maybe it's a Jedi knight!" Burger said. "Remember the way Obi-Wan is dressed in the first *Star Wars*?

That would be cool. Is there a lightsaber in the box? Or a laser gun? Anything?"

Nick turned the box over and a little leather pouch fell out. He undid the drawstring and peered in. "It, um, kind of looks like brown sugar."

Connor let out a desperate laugh. "A monk's robe and a bag of brown sugar? I don't see how that helps us."

"Don't worry, this one will do the trick," Burger said, brandishing his box. "I can feel it."

He opened the box with a flourish and snatched out the contents in one motion, holding the costume up in front of the other two.

It was a small piece of sparkly purple spandex attached to a pink tutu.

"This is not good."

21

NICK AND BURGER RACED DOWN THE COBBLESTONE walkway to the Millards' waterfront house, through driftwood arches and past koi ponds fed by mini-waterfalls. It looked like the entrance to an expensive theme park, but fun was the last thing on the boys' minds.

The plan had changed. Forget the delivery. Focus on evacuation and survival.

When the house finally came into sight, it seemed as if every Southsider in the seventh grade had been invited. A cowboy, two scary clowns, and a school of mermaids sat around a bonfire. A group of superheroes played volleyball. And a bug-eyed alien grilled burgers while a couple of pirates waited in line behind some colorful anime characters.

Twilight came early in the fall, and dozens of tiki torches blazed away along the perimeter of the party, cutting through the oncoming dusk.

Nick and Burger dashed past the torches, knocking into hoboes, cavemen, and an assortment of video-game villains.

"Hey!"

"Watch out."

Nick scanned the grounds and grabbed a nearby Oompa Loompa. "Have you seen Hayley?"

"Nick Stringer—seriously?"

"And is that Burger?"

"What are you two doing here?"

"WHERE'S HAYLEY?"

"Settle down, bro. I think she's up at the house."

Nick and Burger pounded up the brick walkway to the deck. A princess sneered as they ran by.

The deck was lined with bay windows that revealed a living room bigger than Nick's entire house. He ran his eyes over the partygoers on the twisty staircase and hanging over the ledge of the mezzanine.

"There she is." Burger pointed to the granite fireplace, where Hayley sat laughing with a couple of angels and a fireman. She looked like she was supposed to be a nurse, but the nurses Nick had seen at the hospital wore way more clothes than she was wearing.

They opened the sliding-glass door and pushed their way through the mob, until they reached the fireplace.

"Have you seen your brother?" Nick panted. "And his friends?"

"What are *they* doing here?" the fireman said.

"It's cool. They're invited." Hayley turned back to Nick and gave him that cute, crooked grin. She gestured to his trench coat and fedora. "So what are you two supposed to be? Creepy middle-aged guys?"

"It doesn't matter. Have you seen your brother?"

"Relax." Hayley gave him a curious look. "They're down at the guesthouse. I didn't think you'd be real interested in seeing him again, though."

"Where's the guesthouse?" Burger said.

Hayley inclined her head toward the windows. Nick and Burger looked out and saw a cottage on the edge of a bluff overlooking the water.

"How long have they been in there?"

"Why would you possibly care?"

"Hayley—please—just tell us."

She shrugged. "I don't know. An hour, maybe? Look, I'm glad you could come to the party, but that doesn't mean—"

"We need to talk to you, *now*," Nick said, pulling her into a corner. Burger followed behind them. "Where are your parents?"

"My parents?" Hayley rolled her eyes. "Nick, my parents aren't here. That's why we're having the party." She looked over to her concerned group of friends and gave them the *just-a-minute* sign.

Nick held her by the shoulders. "Okay, you have to really listen to me. Ready? Up at the road there's a U-Haul truck. A friend of ours is driving it. We need to get everyone at this party to run up there and get in the back. We'll drive them someplace safe."

"Now." Burger nodded vigorously. "We need to do it now."

Hayley just stared at them for a few moments, eyebrows furrowed in confusion, before she burst out laughing.

"That's a good one. Look, I said you could come to the party, and here you are. Now just try to have fun, okay? Drop the weird stuff."

"Hayley, listen. I will do anything. Write your Biology reports, type up the labs, get you the answers to the final, whatever. Free of charge. Just please listen to me."

"Did Nick Stringer just say 'free of charge'?" Hayley tilted her head and really looked at them. "You two are serious, aren't you?"

Burger nodded some more. "You can trust us. Totally."

She crossed her arms over her chest and blew her hair out of her eyes. "Well, can you at least tell me what's going on?"

Nick and Burger glanced at each other. "There's not a lot of time. And—"

"—it's going to sound crazy at first, but—"

"—basically, your brother and his friends have—"

"Hayley, how did you do that?" A biker gang burst in through the sliding-glass door, chattering excitedly.

"I didn't even see it when we first got here."

"It looks so real!"

"What's it made out of?"

Before Hayley could respond, Nick took off through the door and onto the deck, Burger close behind.

A group of kids stood in a semicircle, examining something. When Nick got closer, he saw a thick silver rope wrapped around one of the balusters of the deck railing. His eyes followed it up to the roof, where a mass of silver ropes crisscrossed each other and spread out, attached to the chimney, the satellite dish, and the gutters, and then dropped down the side of the house, where they were anchored to a row of rhododendron bushes. The thick strands spiraled down into a circle in the middle of the whole thing.

It was the world's biggest spiderweb.

One of the angels got close to the silver rope and stretched out her hand. "Don't touch it!" Nick shouted.

Too late. The girl tried to pull her hand away, but it was stuck fast. "Ewww. It's like superglue."

A few of the bikers tried to pull her away from the web, but it quickly caught them, too. Anything that brushed up against a silver strand—arms, legs, clothes, hair, whatever—became instantly bonded to the web. Soon half a dozen partygoers were trapped.

"What did you put on this thing to make it so super sticky, anyway?"

"Come on. This isn't funny, Hayley."

Nick scanned the surrounding area, his heart beating like crazy, while Burger dashed into the house.

Hayley grabbed on to Nick's arm. "What is going on?"

"I've been trying to tell you, Chet and his friends—"

Burger flew back out on the deck and thrust the poker from the fireplace at Nick. In his other hand he held an oversize kitchen knife. "Dude. We gotta get them outta there."

Nick looked at Hayley. "He's right. Whatever built this web must be close. It'll be back soon."

"What?"

Nick and Burger approached the group caught by the web. The kids had thrashed around, pulling and yanking to get loose, and had gotten tangled up even worse. One of the angels was crying because her gossamer wings had ripped apart.

Burger dropped to his knees and sawed at the silver cord where it latched on to the deck railing, but the knife got mired in the sticky coating and wouldn't budge.

Nick hoisted the poker over his head with both hands, like an ax, and brought it crashing down on the web as hard as he could. Instead of slicing the silver rope in half, it held fast to the material and became impossible to lift for another blow.

More costumed partygoers piled onto the deck, checking out the commotion. Burger yelled to Nick over the increasing din of bewildered conversation, "We need to figure out a way to—"

"AAAAAEEEEEGGHH!" The angel screamed. Nick followed her terrified gaze to the top of the house.

Out from behind the stone chimney came a spider the size of a VW Bug. All of its legs were covered with coarse bristles of hair. As it scrambled across the roof, shingles splintered and fell away.

The crowd froze, all eyes locked on the monster.

The giant tarantula thundered over to the gutter, then leapt an impossible distance through the air to land on the web. Incredibly nimble for its size, the spider scurried down with uncanny balance.

The angel's screams cut off as she fainted, her entire body slumping against the sticky web.

The rest of the kids that were caught strained to escape, but they just got bound even tighter together in a squirming, struggling knot.

When the spider reached the angel, Nick could see its cold black eyes and fangs. It reared up and a thick, gray rope shot out from its stomach and struck the angel, fusing to her costume.

The spider used three of its forelegs to spin the girl's limp body around and around as the gray rope kept spooling out. The angel looked like a rag doll in the grip of the enormous beast. Nick was struck by how utterly helpless she was—how helpless they *all* were in the face of such a monster—and he had to fight off a rising sense of panic.

222

Soon the girl was unrecognizable, completely wrapped up in spider string like a mummy in a cocoon.

That broke the crowd's paralysis. Everyone turned and ran blindly, smashing into each other and tripping across the deck. Drinks were dropped, making the deck a slippery mess.

Then the spider turned and shot a sticky strand at a fleeing biker. Even though he was thrashing and clawing to get away, the biker got wrapped up just as easily as the girl who had passed out. His screams became muffled as the gummy cord looped around his face.

Nick grabbed Hayley. "I need you to focus. You have to help."

To her credit, Hayley didn't freak out. Heck, it was hard enough for Nick to keep it together, and he at least had some idea of what was happening. Instead, she clutched his arm and looked right into his eyes. Even with the chaos swirling around them, that did something funny to Nick's stomach. Although it was difficult, at that particular moment, for him to separate the tingly feeling of making a connection with her from frayed nerves from sheer terror.

Hayley took a deep breath. "What can I do?"

"Gather up as many people as you can and get them to the truck," he called over the panicked screams.

She nodded. More screams from behind them. Nick turned to see what it was, but Hayley held fast for a

moment. "Nick? I don't know what's going on, but thanks for coming to help me and my friends."

One of the windows of the guesthouse exploded, glass shards raining down on the lawn. A bone-chilling howl rose from within.

Nick let go of Hayley, grabbed as many people as he could, and shoved them in the direction of the driveway. He pointed and shouted instructions that got lost in the mass confusion.

A roar came from the cottage, along with a shriek and some loud banging. Two more windows shattered. The front door flew open, a battle-ax buried inches deep in its wood.

"Go!" Nick called to Hayley. "Get everyone who will listen to run up the hill! Now!"

The monsters poured out of the cottage, snarling and howling and chomping.

Hayley gasped. "Nick. Be careful!" she called before disappearing into the rushing mob.

There were still several hours to go before midnight.

"BAYSIDE POLICE DEPARTMENT. HOW MAY I HELP you?"

"I need you to send as many squad cars as possible to 4357 Chuckanut Drive." Connor read the address off the ornate marble sign that welcomed guests to the Millard residence. He sat in the U-Haul at the top of the long, twisty driveway.

"What is the nature of the emergency?"

"Well, it's not technically an emergency. Yet. But it will be soon."

"Can you describe what is happening, sir?"

"Okay, stay with me on this. Please. I, um, have reason to believe that a group of ... monsters ... will be attacking this house in the near future."

There was a pause. "Monsters?"

"Yes, ma'am."

The police dispatcher sighed. "Very funny, sir. I suggest you offer them free candy to avoid any unwanted attacks. That seems to be working out pretty well for other residents this evening."

"No! You have to listen. There really is a group of—"

"Sir, this is one of our busiest nights of the year. Please leave the lines open for someone with an actual emergency. Thank you and have a good night."

The line cut out. Connor just stared out the windshield as darkness settled over Bayside.

What could he do to make them believe him? Show them the crystal-ball phone? Or the wormhole map? Mary Goodwin would no doubt have her revenge, but he had to risk it. He would never be able to live with himself if kids actually died because he had let these costumes fall into the wrong hands.

Connor was still staring through the window when Frankenstein's monster came lurching straight for the truck.

He screamed and dropped the phone, then fumbled for the keys, which fell to the floorboards.

The creature with green skin and bolts sticking out of its bloody neck advanced even faster.

Connor bent in half, lunging his head and shoulders underneath the big steering wheel, looking for the keys. But it was so dark. He spread his hands out and frantically swept them across the floor mats, finally finding the keys just underneath the seat. When he bolted back up, he smacked his head on the bottom of the steering wheel.

Finally he was upright, trying to jam the right key in the ignition, but his hands were shaking so badly that he dropped them again.

BAM! BAM! BAM!

The undead horror was beating on the door.

And right behind him were Dorothy, the Cowardly Lion, Tarzan, Robin Hood, and a nurse. And Nick and Burger.

Connor looked more closely at "Frankenstein." He was barely over five feet tall and his skin looked more pastel than the dull hue of rotting flesh. Just a kid in a costume. A normal costume.

Connor opened his door. "What are you—"

"We have to get them hidden in the cargo bay. Fast." Nick led the group around to the back of the truck. Dorothy and Robin Hood were clutching on to each other, faces pale with fear. Ol' Frankenstein was shaking so badly that it was no wonder Connor mistook him for a newly reanimated corpse learning to walk again.

"What's going on down there?" He pushed the loading door up and open.

The big one, Burger, led the middle schoolers into the back of the truck, speaking soothingly to them. Nick turned his attention to Connor.

"They're here. The guys with the costumes. It's started." The kid's eyes were haunted. "We'll go down again and get as many people as we can and load them up in the back. Then we drive away as fast as this truck will go and keep driving until it runs out of gas."

A roar drifted up from the house down below, followed by a chorus of screams. The kids in the back of the truck shrank against the walls.

"Hayley, come here." Nick held his hand out to the girl in a skimpy nurse costume. She just stared at him. "Trust me."

The girl looked at the other kids in the cargo bay, then slowly got up, took Nick's hand, and stepped out of the back of the truck.

"This is Connor. He's going to help get us out of here, okay? You and me and as many of your friends as we can get up here." Nick took her by the shoulders, more gently this time. "But we still need your help. Okay?"

"Nick, those . . . *things* coming out of the guest cottage. What did they do with my brother and his friends?" She shuddered. "You don't think that they . . . that they actually . . ."

Burger stepped up. "Well, there's good news and bad news about those things."

Hayley looked back and forth between Nick and Burger. Nick nodded. "He's right."

"Okay, what's the good news?"

"They didn't hurt your brother," Burger said. "Or, you know, kill him or maim him or eat him. Or impale him or whatever."

Nick punched him in the shoulder. "Real comforting, Burger."

Hayley bit her lip. "What's the bad news?"

Nick took a deep breath. "Those things didn't hurt your brother and his friends... because those things *are* your brother and his friends."

"*What?*"

"Look, we can't explain right now. We have to get as many people to safety as possible. But I promise to explain everything later, okay?"

Hayley nodded.

"All right. I need you to be in charge of getting people into the truck and calming them down, keeping them quiet. That means you need to be calm, too. Can you do that?"

The girl glanced nervously down the driveway toward the house, but when she looked back at Nick, her eyes were clearer. She nodded.

Nick turned to Connor. "Hayley lives here. If we're not back in ten minutes, take off and she can help navigate. She'll make sure you get away instead of getting stuck on any side roads or logging paths." He took Hayley by the hand and led her to the door on the passenger's side while Burger disappeared into the back of the truck.

After he got her in the truck, Nick hustled back toward the cargo bay, but Hayley unrolled the window and called for him.

"Yeah?"

"Come back soon, Nick."

He looked like he wanted to say something else, but Burger came barreling out of the back of the truck and thrust one of the two boxes he was carrying into Nick's hands.

"Just in case, dude," Burger said.

Nick took a deep breath. "Okay. Let's get down there." He turned to Connor. "Ten minutes. Then take off and don't look back."

The two kids raced away from the truck, heading down the hill to face the monsters.

22

NICK AND BURGER PAUSED ON THE EDGE OF THE cobblestone walkway to catch their breath and survey the scene.

It looked like a dozen different horror movies had been put into a blender, scrambled up together, and then splattered all over the Millard estate.

A snarling werewolf and a moaning zombie advanced on a group of middle schoolers on the front lawn. A few of the partygoers grabbed burning sticks from the bonfire and waved them at their attackers. The werewolf howled as the makeshift torch singed his fur and forced him back a few steps. But the flames were dying out and the sticks would soon go cold. . . .

The sound of cackling laughter drew their attention

to the roof. A living skeleton was chasing a group of kids who had apparently tried to hide up there. The middle schoolers were a little faster—rubber Vans soles offered better traction than bare-bone feet—but they were being herded toward the corner of the roof and would soon be trapped....

A muscular Viking swung his battle-ax while an enormous troll wielded a club, smashing the deck furniture that kids were trying to hide behind. There were only a few lounge chairs left, and then the partygoers would all be pressed up against the deck railing with nowhere to hide....

An evil scarecrow stabbed his pitchfork at a screaming group of kids on the bluff, sending them closer and closer to the edge with each lunge....

The giant spider was busily wrapping up a dozen bodies that it had caught in its web. As soon as it was finished, it would be time to start feasting....

Nick watched the hideous scene unfold and shook his head. "I guess this is our only hope." He pulled the plain brown robe out of his garment box and held it up. "I just wish I knew what it was before I put it on."

"Maybe you'd be, like, a healer or something. And the brown-sugar stuff is your medicine or potion or whatever. That could help."

"I was hoping for something more along the lines of Gandalf or Dumbledore. You know, magic fighting powers?"

A fresh batch of screams rose up from the Halloween war zone.

Nick took a deep breath and threw on the robe.

His skin went soft and wrinkly and the hairs on his arm turned white. His limbs stiffened up and his joints started to ache. His back became stooped and his knees went shaky.

"Oh, man. No. That's not going to help," Burger said.

"What?" Nick's voice was creaky. Dusty.

"You're just *old*." Burger gestured at Nick's withered body. "You're an old, old man."

A collective gasp went up from the mob on top of the house. A kid in an astronaut costume had slipped and was dangling off the edge of the roof, desperately gripping on to the gutter. The skeleton threw its skull face back and shrieked with laughter.

With a groaning creak of twisted metal, the gutter came loose section by section and the astronaut plunged three stories and crashed in the rhododendron bushes.

"Come on!" Burger raced down the hill. Nick tried to follow, but his tired feet got caught up in the robe and sent him sprawling to the ground. His body felt brittle and broken as it crashed onto the cobblestones. It hurt too much to stand back up.

A few moments later he was grabbed around the shoulders and pulled to his feet. "Let's go," Burger said. "If you're a healer or a wizard or whatever, then that astronaut needs you." Nick put his arm around Burger's meaty shoulders for support and they made their way down the hill as screams continued to rain down from the roof.

The astronaut's helmet had popped off and he was moaning in pain, writhing around in the bushes and clutching his ankle.

When he saw Nick, his eyes went wide and he tried to scramble away, but he was caught in the branches and just ended up thrashing around and crying out in pain.

"It's okay," Nick wheezed. He reached out toward the boy. "We're trying to help."

But the astronaut continued flailing, trying to back away and tangling himself even worse, his cries becoming screams as he clutched at his injured leg.

"He's probably in shock," Nick said. "Thinks I'm one of the creepies. Try to calm him down while I get out this pouch of stuff, see if it helps."

Nick pulled out the little bag, grabbed a handful of the brown sugar, and flung it at the astronaut.

The screaming cut off instantly. The boy went limp.

"Oh, crap! Did I kill him?"

The astronaut's body sagged among the branches, unmoving.

"Seriously, did I—"

"Zzzzzzzzz."

Nick and Burger looked at each other. "...Is he *sleeping?*"

They crept closer. The astronaut's body was turned toward the sky, a goofy grin plastered on his face as he snored deeply. A trickle of drool ran out the side of his mouth. He was *out*.

"Dude!"

"What?"

"You're the Sandman."

The boys looked down at the pouch full of magic sleepy-sand, then up at the skeleton as it scrambled across the roof, bones clacking against the shingles. The group of middle schoolers was huddled up along the edge, their feet only inches away from where the gutter had been ripped off.

"Remember what happened when you fell asleep in the ghost costume?"

Burger nodded. "It stopped working. We have to get you up there. Now."

"Burger, I'm way too old to move that fast." Nick reached out a wrinkled hand and pointed to the sparkly costume in Burger's grip. "Time for you to put that on."

"What? No way. What would I do, ballet-dance the monsters to death?"

Nick took the costume out of Burger's grip and flipped it over. "Look. You have wings."

Burger groaned and rolled his eyes. "Are you serious?"

The kids up top screamed again. A girl in a lifeguard costume had almost fallen off the roof, and a surfer dude had a hold on her arm as she teetered at the edge.

Nick thrust the sparkly spandex at Burger. "Put it on, big fella. See if you can get me up there in time."

Burger sighed and started to pull the costume over his head. "At least it'll be fun to fly, right?"

Even though the spandex was super stretchy, Burger's body tested its limits. He shrugged and shimmied, trying to get it over his shoulders and chest. Nick grabbed with both hands and pulled as hard as he could until—

Poof!

"Burger?" Nick wheezed. "Where did you go? Are you invisible again?"

"No," came a squeaky voice. "I'm right here."

Nick looked around. And there, hovering in midair with wings whirring like a hummingbird, was Burger. The costume fit much better now that he was less than a foot tall. Although the necklace made of flower petals and all of the silver glitter still looked out of place on him, no matter what size he was.

"Oh, look. It's little Burgerbell the magical fairy."

"Shut up, old man," Burger peeped. He lunged forward and punched Nick in the shoulder.

"Ouch! You're pretty strong for such a cute little sprite."

"Let's see if it does us any good."

Burger buzzed around behind Nick, grabbed the shoulders of his brown robe in two tiny fists, and squeak-grunted as he launched himself skyward.

Nick gasped as he rose straight up in the air, past the windows on all three floors, and reached the roof.

The middle schoolers cringed in fright as Old Man Nick zoomed up until he was level with them. They edged away from him, which only put them nearer to the skeleton, who was gathering itself for a leap at the crowd.

"It's okay!" Burger peeped as loudly as he could. "We're the rescue team."

"Get down!" Nick shouted. "Now!" He gestured emphatically, lowering both palms to the roof.

The middle schoolers got the hint and dropped to their knees and stomachs just as the skeleton dove forward, his bony fingers gnarled into claws and his mouth wide open to tear into flesh. Nick gathered up a handful of sand as Burgerbell flew him forward.

The skeleton was in midflight when the sand hit it in the face, disappearing into its gaping eye- and nose-holes.

When it crashed to the roof, there was a much bigger thud than bones alone could have made. Nick looked down and saw the wiry, black-haired football player. He was conked out on the roof, snoring away, with a skeleton costume draped across his body.

Burgerbell set Old Man Nick down on the shingles. "That was awesome," he squeaked.

Nick turned to the terrified crowd of kids huddling together. "Listen very carefully," he intoned in his deep old-man voice. He pointed up toward the road. "There's a U-Haul truck up at the top of the driveway. Go up there and Hayley will help you get in the back and take you someplace safe."

The middle schoolers slowly stood back up.

"Who are you?" a kid in a prisoner outfit asked.

"We're the good guys," Nick said.

"Yeah." Burger stood as tall as he could on Nick's shoulder, his sparkly purple chest puffed out with pride as he looked out across the chaos raging across the Millard estate. "And we have work to do."

22½

"HAS IT BEEN TEN MINUTES YET?" DOROTHY
asked. She was nuzzled up to the Cowardly Lion, trembling with fright or cold or both.

"Keep your voice down," Hayley whispered. She and Connor had joined the middle schoolers in the back of the truck, trying to keep everyone calm and quiet. Connor closed the loading door of the U-Haul, on the slim chance of remaining hidden if any monsters showed up. "And we're not leaving yet. We have to wait for more people to get here first. We're going to save as many as we can."

Connor Flanagan leaned over the back of the seat and shined his flashlight on the dashboard clock. "They still have a few minutes," he said. He wanted to think of something else—anything else—that he could say to these kids to help them stay calm. But that was difficult when he was so terrified himself.

He sat back down, the cold of the cargo-bay floor seeping through his pants and making him shiver.

The kids sat in a circle on the floor of the storage area. It was hard to tell if the muffled wails that made it through the truck's walls were emanating from the party or just the sound of the wind blowing through the trees.

Connor tried to focus on the task at hand: wait for ten minutes, then carefully drive away if he needed to, getting as many kids to safety as possible. This helped distract his mind from dwelling on the fallout. How many kids would get hurt tonight? Or worse—killed? What would the police do when they found the costumes? And what would Mary Goodwin do when she found out that—

Smash!

A pale hand burst right through the roof of the truck.

The fingers, with sharp nails like talons, spread out and got a grip. Then, with a terrible screeching of shredded metal, an entire section of the roof was ripped away, revealing a sky full of moon and stars.

The thing that dropped down into the storage area was dressed stylishly, all in black, which served to make his face look even more inhumanly white.

Tall and lean with slicked-back hair, he tilted his head to the side, closed his eyes with a dreamy expression on his face, and inhaled deeply. "Mmmmmmm. Smells delicious in here."

When he smiled, his long fangs glistened in the moonlight now shining through the new hole in the roof.

He lowered his head and fixed each of the kids in turn with bloodred eyes, before finally settling on Hayley.

"Hey, Sis."

23

NICK WAS LYING AT THE BASE OF THE SPIDERWEB, eyes closed, legs splayed, and head cocked at a weird angle, as if he had passed out and collapsed there. Burger was the hidden lookout, nestled in the folds of the robe's hood with just his little fairy eyes peeking out.

"Wait for it. . . ." Burger peep-whispered. "Wait for it. . . ."

Nick could feel the deck shudder underneath him as the giant spider thundered down the web toward his body. It took all of his willpower to remain still and wait for Burger's signal.

Just before one of those hairy legs stabbed his chest, Burger shouted, "Now!"

As fast as his tired old bones would allow, Nick scooped a handful of magic sand and threw it in the spider's face.

An instant later another Bayside football player was crashed out on the deck, snoring and drooling, draped in a dark eight-legged costume.

The silver strands of the web melted, leaving a dozen bodies strewn about the deck covered in slick, gooey residue.

"Ewww." The angel stood up, wiping globs of gummy giant-spider silk off her arms and legs. "Disgusting."

"Hey, at least it's better than being eaten alive," Burger squeaked indignantly as he buzzed around Nick's head.

The newly freed group of partygoers huddled around the sleeping football player. A kid in a Fat Elvis costume pointed at him. "That's just Derek Kamphouse. My sister used to go out with him."

One of the bikers who had been trapped in the web picked up the spider costume and turned it over in his hands, examining it. "What is going on?" Then he turned his attention to the old man and the flying fairy. "And who the heck are you?"

Burger crossed his little arms over his sparkly chest. "A *thank-you* would be nice."

"It doesn't matter," Nick wheezed. "You all need to go up to the main road. Hayley is there with a U-Haul truck. She's going to take everyone far away from here. You need to go now, before—"

Fresh screams rose up from the lower deck. Everyone rushed to the railing and leaned over.

All of the deck furniture in the area had been reduced to piles of kindling. The Viking and troll were chasing partygoers all over, swinging their weapons with abandon.

The Viking lumbered after a girl in a cheerleader costume, and his sword came crashing down just inches from her foot. Splinters flew up upon impact, and the Viking had to pause and wrench his sword free from the wood. Nick cringed—a blow that strong would have taken a foot clean off. The cheerleader raced away, but there were still plenty of kids around when the Viking was on the move again.

"We have to get down there," peeped Burger.

A few kids turned and hurried off in the direction of the driveway, following Nick's instructions, but the biker gang stepped forward.

"We want to help."

Nick and Burger looked at each other, deciding together in the silent way that only best friends can. Burger, standing on top of the deck railing but still not as tall as the others, nodded his little head.

Nick looked at the bikers. "Okay, here's the deal: I need to get really close to them so I can do my thing." He held up the bag of magic sand. "But I can't move very fast, obviously."

"And if he gets hit by that sword or club, it's all over," Burger chimed in.

"I have an idea," the tallest biker said. "Maybe we can bring them to you, instead."

He laid out his plan. Nick and Burger looked at each other again. "That could work."

"It's worth a shot."

Nick made his way down the stairs to the lower deck and crouched against the wall, his brown robe blending in with the wood as the mob rushed by.

The bikers dashed over to a koi pond and collected handfuls of rocks that lined the pool.

Burger flew right down into the middle of the action, buzzing in the faces of the Viking and the troll. They paused to brush the sparkly little disturbance out of their eyes, which bought everyone a few moments of time.

But then the troll's hand shot out and he grabbed Burger in one green fist. Nick gasped. That was not part of the plan.

The troll held Burger up to his face, squinting at the little fairy. He sniffed a few times. Burger squirmed in his grip and beat at the green fingers with his tiny fists, but it didn't do any good.

"Food?" the trolled grumbled. He stretched his mouth wide and lifted Burger, headfirst, ready to take a bite.

A rock bounced off one of his oversize yellow teeth.

The troll roared in pain. Another rock ricocheted off his nose, and two more smacked into his forehead.

The beast grunted and dropped Burger, looking around for his attackers.

In the middle of the deck stood the biker gang, firing rocks at the troll. The rest of the kids fanned out and pressed themselves against the railing, leaving the big deck wide open.

The Viking had a group of kids trapped in the corner of the deck. A volley of rocks clanged off his horned helmet and thudded against his leather vest. He turned around and bellowed in rage.

The bikers held their ground in the center of the deck, firing rock after rock at the invaders.

With a great war cry, the Viking charged. The troll followed, hoisting his club above his head with both hands.

Somehow the bikers held ranks, standing there and firing rocks while the roaring attackers charged.

At the last moment, the gang turned and fled as a group, the Viking and troll close behind them. The kids raced straight for the crouching Nick.

Burger flew over them and grabbed Nick's robe, helping him leap to his feet at just the right moment. The biker gang took a sharp turn, and their war-whooping attackers didn't even notice Nick as he reached into his pouch and flung two handfuls of sand.

The Viking and troll collapsed. An instant later it was just Ox and another football player taking a nap on the deck. The horned helmet was way too big for Ox's head, making him look like a little kid playing dress-up with his dad's clothes.

Everyone on the deck came over to check out the fallen foes.

"It was just those guys?"

"For real?"

The angels were all staring at Burger as he buzzed around Nick's shoulders. "This can't be happening," one of them said.

"What is going on?"

"Is this, like, virtual reality or something?" A guy in a toga squinted and waved his arms out in front of him, apparently testing this version of reality for glitches. "You know, a simulation?"

"No, it's real." Nick stooped over and picked up both costumes and held them in the air. "These are responsible. So don't mess with Ox or any of the other football players, okay? Just let them sleep it off. They didn't mean to hurt you."

He turned to one of the bikers. "Can you carry these up to the U-Haul? Make sure *nobody* tries to put them on. Just give them to the driver. We'll be up soon."

"Wait a minute." The biker pointed over the deck to the lawn. "There are only three of them left." The werewolf, zombie, and evil scarecrow had herded the last group of kids up against the edge of the bluff. "And there are a lot more of us."

There were partygoers coming from the upper deck and climbing down from the roof. Still others emerged from various hiding places throughout the house and yard.

Soon the deck was full of middle schoolers. Nick looked out over the crowd. "It might be dangerous. But who wants to fight?"

Every hand went up in the air.

23½

CONNOR FLANAGAN MUSTERED UP THE LAST
shreds of his courage and placed himself between the
vampire and the kids.

"Don't touch them," he said. Not knowing what to do
next, he awkwardly put both fists in front of his face like
an old-timey bare-knuckle brawler, even though he had
never been in a fight.

The vampire just laughed. And then he moved so
quickly that Connor didn't even see him. One moment
he was standing in the middle of the cargo bay with his
arms crossed over his chest, and the next instant he had
his icy hand around Connor's throat. He easily hoisted
Connor in the air and slammed him against the metal
wall.

"I don't care about these kids." His voice was as raspy as dead leaves blowing across concrete.

"Put him down. Please," Hayley said. When he didn't respond, she added, "Chet? Is that really you?"

"Actually, no." The vampire laughed again. "I'm something much better than Chet now." He casually tossed Connor, who went flying through the air and smashed into the loading door. The kids on the ground whimpered and cringed against the wall.

The vampire strutted around the back of the truck. "Maybe you notice something a little different about me?"

Hayley nodded. "I know, Chet. You can walk now. That's great. But you really don't want to hurt anybody in here."

"Oh, please. I can do much more than just walk." He stomped around the cargo bay before pivoting on one leg and kicking a hole right through the thick metal wall. Then he effortlessly kicked another hole. And another one. It looked like the U-Haul had been attacked with cannonballs.

The vampire crouched, gathering himself, and leapt into the air and out the hole in the roof. A few moments later he dropped back down, landing with perfect balance. He brushed off his sleek black cape and gestured at his new legs with a flourish. "Finding those costumes is the best thing that ever happened to me."

"What do you want?" Connor was rubbing his head, still crumpled in a heap against the door. He tried to push himself up, collect his thoughts, but his head had taken a pretty nasty blow.

"Oh, what I want is real simple." Chet strolled over to Connor and bent so they were eye to eye. "You are going to take me to wherever those costumes come from."

Connor shook his head. "I don't know what you're talking about."

"Wrong answer!" With his lightning speed, the vampire hoisted Connor over his head, pinning the delivery-man's back against the ceiling. Then he let go and Connor went crashing to the metal floor.

Hayley crawled over and placed herself between Connor and the vampire. "Leave him alone, Chet. Please. He never did anything to you."

"Oh, but he did. He just lied to me." The vampire's eyes flashed even redder, glowing embers of hate set deep in that bone-white flesh. He picked up an empty garment box and waved it in the air. "This costume came in a box just like this." Pointing a sharp talon at Connor, he said, "Which means he knows where I'll be able to find more. A lifetime supply, I bet."

"Chet, you're not yourself. You don't know what you're—"

"This is my *new* self!" He screamed it, his raspy voice breaking. The vampire charged around the cargo bay, out of control, kicking a series of new holes in the sides of the U-Haul. "I can do anything now!" The truck shuddered and rocked while the kids wrapped their heads in their hands and curled into the fetal position.

The vampire turned and advanced on Hayley. "Don't you get it?" He dropped to one knee and grimaced at her, fangs slipping out of his mouth and curving over his bottom lip. "I. Will. NEVER. Use. That. Wheelchair. Again."

Hayley was trembling all over and her voice was shaky, but she forged ahead. "Chet, you don't want to—"

"Chet is dead!" he snarled. Then the vampire picked up Connor by the scruff of the neck with one hand, carried him across the length of the cargo bay, and threw him over the seats to crash into the dashboard. "Now drive us to wherever those costumes come from."

Connor picked himself up off the floorboards, wiping blood off of his bruised forehead.

"At least let the kids go first."

"I don't think so." The vampire shook his head slowly and grinned. "I'm starting to get hungry. I might need some snacks on the way."

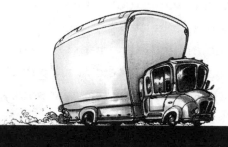

THE LAST THREE MONSTERS COULDN'T PUT UP much of a fight with an army of middle schoolers charging at them.

The partygoers swarmed over the werewolf, the evil scarecrow, and the zombie. There were enough kids for four or five of them to grab hold of each of the monsters' arms and legs, and soon the monsters were immobilized and swallowed up by the crowd. Then they were marched, snarling and moaning, before the Sandman, who promptly put them all to sleep.

Nick exhaled slowly and it felt like the first time he had done so in days. He pulled off the brown robe and felt his own, youthful energy surge back through his body.

The crowd gasped as he changed from centuries-old man back into boy.

Burgerbell stood on Nick's shoulder and waved to everyone, then started to peel off the purple spandex.

"No, wait—" Nick said, but it was too late. Burger turned back into himself, and Nick crumpled underneath the full form of his friend.

But the crowd didn't laugh. When Nick and Burger stood up and brushed themselves off, everyone was gazing at them, wide-eyed. Nick didn't see who started the applause, but others followed and soon everyone was clapping and cheering like crazy. Two of the angels rushed up and hugged Burger. The bikers fist-bumped Nick and pounded him on the back. Everyone poured out a million questions and compliments.

Nick allowed himself a moment to stand there and soak up their adoration. But there was still a little work to be done.

He waded through the crowd to a grinning Burger, who looked like he could have hung out there and soaked in the praise-bath all night.

"Come on, we need to go tell Connor that he doesn't need to leave."

They broke away from the mob, but halfway up the walkway they met some of the kids who had been on the roof with the spider. They were running back to the house.

"What's going on?"

A kid in a hillbilly costume stopped, trying to catch his breath. "That truck we were supposed to get on? It took off. The roof was all torn apart and we could hear people screaming inside."

Nick and Burger looked at each other. "Chet." They both said it at the same time.

"Everything was so crazy I totally forgot about keeping track of who was popping out of those costumes."

"Me, too."

"What are we going to do?"

The hillbilly was walking away, but Nick grabbed him. "Do you know if the Millards keep any bikes around here?"

"There might be some in the garage," he said before racing on.

"Follow me," Nick said. "I think I have a plan."

The boys rode the borrowed bikes down the hidden trail as quickly as they dared to in the dark, following the shaky beam of Nick's flashlight.

When they reached the delivery truck it looked eerie in the moonlight, lying on its side in the middle of the forest. The boys jumped off their bikes and picked their way across the clearing until they came to the dragon costume stretched out on the ground.

Its green tail was trapped underneath the fallen tree,

but the earth was soft from weeks of rain and easy to dig up with bare hands. They soon pulled the tail out from underneath the trunk and freed the whole costume.

Burger wiped sweat and mud off his forehead with the back of his hand. "Okay, dude. I totally don't mind getting in there if we can save Connor and Hayley and everyone. But what if it messes with us? Connor tried to kill us in this thing, and he's one of the nicest guys I've ever—"

"That's not my plan." Nick gathered the dragon head in both arms, then marched over and climbed on top of the truck.

"What are you doing up there?"

Nick spread his palms out, the moonlight shimmering on the scales. "Remember the lawn mower? And the robot costume?"

Realization dawned on Burger and he slowly grinned. "You're a genius."

"Me? No way. I got the idea from you, my man."

Burger laughed. "Then we're a genius. Let's do this."

Burger climbed on top of the truck and the boys hooked the corner of the dragon's lips around one edge of the vehicle, then stretched the entire mouth wide. With Nick's help they pulled the costume over the chassis, inch by inch. It looked like the dragon was swallowing the whole thing, boa constrictor–style.

Before they had the costume even halfway on, the dragon stirred and snorted. Clouds of steam poured out of its nostrils as it sat up on its haunches and studied the boys. Nick and Burger dove behind the fallen tree for safety.

When they worked up the nerve to peek back over the trunk, the dragon was still sitting in the middle of the clearing, calmly looking at them.

"I think it's waiting for a driver," Nick said.

"What's that noise?" whispered Burger. "It almost sounds like it's purring."

Nick grinned. "I think that's a cross between a truck engine and a dragon breathing." He climbed over the trunk. "Come on. Let's figure out how to steer this thing."

CONNOR FLANAGAN KEPT HIS EYES TRAINED ON the twisty hilltop road as he carefully steered the U-Haul. Hayley sat in the passenger seat beside him, stealing glances at her brother in the cargo bay.

Glancing at the dashboard clock for the hundredth time didn't make it move any faster. It was only eight thirty. Could he keep the vampire from eating these kids before the costume's power ran out at midnight? Chet was stomping around back there, kicking more holes in the walls and becoming increasingly agitated.

The monster wasn't wearing a seat belt. What if Connor swerved the truck to the side, smashed it into the rocks? The seat belts would protect him and Hayley, but the vampire would get tossed around pretty good, maybe even knocked unconscious. He could try to—

No. No good. The kids in the back weren't wearing seat belts, either. Time to think of a new plan.

He looked at the clock yet again. Eight thirty-one.

"Step on it," the vampire snarled, his fangs mere inches from Connor's neck as he leaned over the seat to look at the speedometer. "You're going ten miles under the speed limit." A cold hand gripped Connor's shoulder, talons digging through his shirt and into his skin, and it was all he could do not to cry out in agony. "The next time you try to play any tricks, one of these kids gets thrown out the back."

Connor nudged the speedometer back up, trying to block out the sounds of the whimpers and sobs coming from the terrified kids in the cargo bay. The vampire retreated to the back again, stalking around to revel in his powerful new legs.

Connor felt a tapping on his arm. He glanced over at Hayley. She laid one finger across her lips to signal for quiet, then pointed through the windshield, up in the air.

Slowly, trying not to broadcast what he was doing, Connor leaned forward and craned his neck to look up.

Hurtling down from out of the sky, weaving back and forth like a drunken sailor, was a very familiar-looking green dragon.

25

"STOP PULLING SO HARD!"

"If you'd just pull harder, we'd be fine."

"Turn right, turn right. No, that's *left*! What's wrong with you?"

"We need instruction manuals!"

Nick and Burger sat on the dragon's neck, each holding on to one of the long green ears and using them to steer like the reins of a horse. But they were spaced so far apart that it was a two-man job.

The steering worked okay, but they hadn't been able to figure out speed control. Ever since the dragon lifted off the ground, it had been zooming through the sky at breakneck speed, individual trees down below lost in a green-and-brown blur.

They swerved back and forth, following the contours of the hilltop road, as they looked out for the U-Haul.

And there it was, finally, twisting and turning along the road carved into the edge of the cliff.

"Dive!" Burger yelled.

Pulling back on the ears made the dragon lift into the air, so they lifted them up and pushed them forward. Sure enough, the scaly beast plummeted down to the road.

Nick had to stand up to see over the top of the dragon's head. "Steady…steady…okay, a little over your way… a little more…No! Not that much!"

"Stop yelling at me!"

Nick slipped on the scales, yanking the ear the wrong way as he held on for dear life. The dragon lurched sickeningly to the side, and Nick's stomach flip-flopped as it felt like he was about to fall off.

Burger grimaced and leaned the other way, pulling as hard as he could on the green ear he was holding. The dragon roared in protest but righted itself, heading straight for the U-Haul.

The flying beast landed with a crash on top of the truck, the claws on all four feet punching right through the roof to get a grip. It was about twice as big as the U-Haul, so its tail draped over the back while its head and shoulders jutted out past the hood. The dragon rode the truck down the twisty road like a skateboard.

"Come on," Nick yelled over the roar of the rushing wind in their ears. "Let's get everyone home."

Burger nodded. The boys pulled back on the ears and the dragon launched into the air, the truck dangling from its grip.

When the dragon dropped out of the sky and landed on the volleyball court in Hayley's backyard, it was instantly surrounded by all of the middle school partygoers. Burger stood on the scaly back, waving while the crowd cheered.

Nick looked at Burger and smiled. He thought they both could probably get used to being noticed a little bit more.

The boys hopped down from the dragon and cleared a path through the crowd to the back of the truck.

"All right, Chet," Nick called through one of the holes that had been kicked through the loading door. "It's time to come out and take that costume off. You're way outnumbered."

"Yeah, and your buddies have all had their costumes removed," Burger added. "Permanently." More cheers went up from the crowd.

A group of groggy football players was led to the front of the crowd. Ox nodded at Nick and Burger. "Hey, guys. We're sorry about, you know . . . trying to hack everybody into little pieces or whatever."

"We've been in the costumes," Burger said. "We know what it's like."

Ox gestured with one of his big arms at the crowd. "They said you told 'em not to mess with me after that stupid costume came off." He shrugged. "So, thanks."

"If you want to pay us back, you can start by talking to your friend in there." Nick gestured toward the truck. "He's still caught up in one of those things."

Ox nodded again. "Hey, Chet," he called, "why don't you come out and take that thing—"

The loading door shot up. "Stand back," the vampire snarled. He was holding Hayley in front of him, shielding himself from the crowd, one of his razor-sharp talons pressed into her neck. "Anyone tries anything and she gets it."

The crowd shrank back, but Nick slowly stepped forward, palms out in what he hoped was a calming gesture. "Chet, you don't want to hurt your sister."

"Stop calling me that." The vampire sneered, revealing his fangs. "Chet is gone."

"No, he's not. He's still in there, and he's better than this. *You're* better than this."

Burger stepped forward and stood with his friend. "Dude. It's fun to be somebody else for a while. We get it. But those costumes will seriously mess with your head."

"It's not my head that I care about," Chet snarled. "No one is going to take these legs away from me. I'm never sitting in that stupid chair again."

"Chet, listen to me." Hayley spoke very slowly, her neck brushing up against those sharp claws. "Nobody cares about your chair. It's not like it slows you down or anything—haven't you noticed?"

"She's right, bro." Ox stepped up next to Nick. "You totally throw the best parties, and you're always cracking the guys up. I mean, you can even bench-press more than me. I don't even notice that chair half the time." The rest of the high schoolers nodded in solidarity.

Chet's face twisted up with conflicting emotions. Nick recognized the feeling from having been in the costumes himself: the real Chet was doing battle with the will of the costume. Who would come out on top? Which was stronger? Hayley's life might depend on the answer.

Nick wondered if there was anything he could do to tip the scale. There must be something he could say to remind Chet of who he really was, what was really important. Some sort of insight he had gained from losing himself in the costumes that would help him connect with the person struggling inside that vampire getup. What if he tried to reason with Chet, told him that—

Connor stepped out from behind the monster, lifted the crystal-ball phone in both hands, and conked the vampire in the back of the head with it.

The monster crumpled to the ground. And then it was just Chet lying there, unconscious, his withered legs covered by a black cape.

"Sorry." Connor shrugged. "But I didn't think we had time for all of that."

26

NICK AND HAYLEY SAT ON THE DECK AS CONNOR and Burger helped some partygoers load the costumes into the back of his delivery truck. The dragon costume was spread out on the volleyball court. Several of the middle schoolers surrounded it, bent over on hands and knees, examining every stitch and green scale. Nick had a feeling that he and Burger were going to be answering a lot of questions over the next few weeks.

Connor had been worried about the big secret getting out like this, and what kind of fallout he'd face back home. But Nick was quick to reassure him. First, it's not like any grown-ups were going to believe such a wild story from a bunch of kids. After all, there was going to be no evidence left behind, and Halloween was the biggest night of the year for pranks. Second—and more important—no kids were going to tell any grown-ups anyway, because they would have to admit they were at a party at the Millards' place with no adult supervision. If they told, they'd get grounded. So it was a matter of mutually assured destruction. Sure, the gossip and the rumors would swirl around for a while, but it would eventually become more myth than fact.

Nick watched as the costumes disappeared into the cargo bay. It was a good thing that the dragon had been able to get the truck out of the woods, because the U-Haul was pretty much smashed beyond all use. Nick would have to add its replacement cost to Connor's expense report, the report he would be submitting to Mary Goodwin. He had a feeling Connor's interaction with that woman was going to change, especially if Nick had anything to do with it.

"So, you guys are still going through with the delivery? After all of that?" Hayley said.

Nick nodded. He had filled her in on most of the details. "Connor made a promise to his dad, and he wants to keep it. I get that."

She gently prodded him in the ribs with her elbow. "Plus, the money should be good, right?"

"Okay, I guess there is that." He grinned sheepishly. "You know, if you think about it, most of the drama was our fault in the first place. And your brother and his friends didn't help, of course. But apparently Connor's family has been making these deliveries for hundreds of years without any problems."

"Okay, but isn't he worried about, like, *unleashing* dangerous stuff into the world? You said it's more than just costumes, right?"

"Let's keep that between us, okay?" He looked around to make sure no one could hear them. "But if this lady, or witch, or whatever she is—if she's making magical stuff and turning a profit on it, I can't think of a better guy than Connor to be in charge of delivering the goods. I mean, he's really responsible. He called the police to try to save everyone at your party, even though he'd have to pay a steep price when he got back home."

Down below, Connor closed the loading door on the truck, and the middle schoolers turned their attention to cleaning up the grounds. The aftermath of the monster massacre was pretty messy.

"I'm sorry we ruined your party," Nick said.

"Are you kidding? People will still be talking about this little get-together when we're all in college." Hayley grinned at him. "I'm sure it was way better than Tania Hillington's princess-themed party."

"You might have a point there."

They sat in easy silence for a while, watching everyone down on the lawn.

"Seriously, though, thanks for everything," Hayley said. "You saved my life. Twice."

"Not to mention your Biology grade."

Hayley sighed. "I never should have asked you to do that."

"Don't worry about it." Nick shrugged. "Besides, I don't think I'm going to be doing that kind of thing anymore."

"No?"

"There are other ways to make money. Better ways." He grinned. "Besides, if I keep cheating for you and Burger, what are you going to do when you get to high school?"

"You might be out of business, anyway." Hayley gestured to the middle schoolers on the lawn. "After tonight, I don't think people are going to see you as that guy anymore, you know?" She smiled shyly at him. "I know that's not how I see you."

"Really? And how do you see me now?"

She raised one eyebrow. "As someone I'd like to invite over again. Get to know better. Without the bribes, this time."

Nick grinned. "Can it maybe be sometime when your brother and his friends aren't around?"

She laughed. "Let's shake on it." She reached out and took his hand. And then she didn't let go.

So he was actually holding hands. With Hayley Millard. That was cooler, by far, than anything that had happened to him in the costumes.

They sat and talked and laughed for a while. Burger joined them, accompanied by his angel admirers. His new friends were enthralled as Burger told them what it was like to ride on the back of a dragon, reenacting the experience with elaborate hand gestures and sound effects. They laughed and clapped at all the right places, and Burger soaked all of it up. And he was already adding details to the story that never happened.

Eventually, Connor made his way up onto the deck.

"I should get going, guys. Thanks for, you know, everything."

"You sure you don't want us to help you make the delivery?" Burger said.

"No, I've got it. Probably good for me to finish up this first one by myself."

"First one?" Nick said. "So that does mean you're going to make a career out of it?"

Connor shrugged. "I guess that depends."

"Depends on what?"

He looked over to where the middle schoolers surrounded the dragon costume. "Well, I'm hoping there's one more thing you can help me with afterward."

Epilogue

THE DRAGON BURST THROUGH THE WORMHOLE north of Salem, Massachusetts, and cruised low over the forested hills. Connor Flanagan navigated by moonlight, following the roads he had driven two nights ago.

When he finally dropped down to the ground, steering the dragon to a clear landing spot through the trees, Mary Goodwin came scrambling out of her shack.

"And just what is all this?" She marched right over, shaking a walking staff up at Connor. "I told you not to go fooling around with the merchandise."

The dragon growled low in its throat and snorted once at the woman, a tendril of smoke curling from its nostrils. Mary Goodwin shrank back, the unease evident on her face. "Easy, boy," Connor said, patting the scales on the back of its neck.

When the dragon settled, the woman took a cautious step forward and lifted her staff again. "What is the meaning of this?"

"I'm afraid it was unavoidable." Connor hopped to the ground. Now that he wasn't cringing in fear before her, he noticed how much taller he was than Mary Goodwin. "Just a necessary part of doing business. And I'd appreciate it if you'd stop waving that stick in my face."

She rocked backward as if slapped.

"A 'necessary part of doing business,' was it? I swear, no member of the Flanagan clan has every spoken to me in such an uppity way." She turned her head and spat a dark blob on the ground. "So do you have any other *demands* you'd like to make?"

Although her words were dripping with sarcasm, Connor answered in earnest. "Actually, yes. I'd like you to meet my business partners."

"WHAT?!" The skin cascaded down her face in lumps and folds. She hastily pushed it back into place.

Nick and Burger stepped out from behind the dragon wings and jumped down to the ground. They strode confidently over to the woman.

"Hello, I'm Nick Stringer, and this is my associate, Mr. Hindberg." He stuck out his hand for a shake, but Mary Goodwin regarded it with a sneer.

"I don't know what you think you're doing, boy," she said to Connor, "but the Flanagans don't have *business partners*. They do what I tell 'em to do and that's that. Always has been."

"Yes, I understand you've all been working under that agreement for some time, now. The better part of three centuries?" Nick wouldn't allow her to ignore him.

She glared at him. "That's none of your affair. If you two don't get out—"

"We believe the time is long overdue for a new arrangement." Nick pulled a piece of paper out of his jeans pocket and handed it to the woman. "One that represents the best interests of all concerned parties."

Mary Goodwin, stunned into silence, looked over the sheet of paper. As she read, her mouth set into a scowl and the wrinkles appeared again, slowly, sliding like glue down her cheeks.

While she was occupied, Connor and Burger unzipped the dragon costume and pulled away the scaly green material, slowly revealing the delivery truck underneath.

The old woman shook her head, newly loose flesh jiggling all over. "Oh, no." She waved the paper dismissively. "No way in Hades am I agreeing to this."

"That's fine." Nick smiled. "My guess is that you need Connor a lot more than he needs you. So if you'd like to retain his services, he'll need everything outlined in this contract, which as you'll see includes a much bigger share of the profits. And, of course, you'll be handing over all of the deeds and titles to his family's property." Nick calmly paced back and forth a bit as he spoke, hands clasped behind his back, clearly in his element. "If you wish to terminate your business relationship, Connor would be more than happy to pursue a career in the dental-care arts. Best of luck to you in finding another trustworthy, loyal clan of human familiars to do your bidding." Nick turned and started to walk back to the truck.

Mary Goodwin trembled with rage, her lumpy flesh turning red. She waved her hand at the little knoll behind her shack and the hill split in two, revealing the torchlit cavern within. "Get out here!" she screeched.

An enormous mud-creature stumbled out from the cave, dripping dead leaves and patches of old moss.

"Take care of them!" Mary Goodwin pointed to the boys.

"Just stand your ground," Nick whispered to the others.

"Are you sure about this?" Connor said as the moaning creature lurched into the clearing, plodding along on blocklike feet of clay and earth.

Nick nodded. "It's a golem. We read about them in Language Arts. Don't worry about it."

Burger shrugged and looked at Connor. "He's crazy-smart. I'd trust him."

The mud-beast staggered closer, looming high above the trio by the delivery truck. It reached out with massive arms and scooped up Burger, holding him like a new-born. Connor started to reach out to grab him, but Nick put a hand on his arm. "Just wait a sec."

The golem turned, carried Burger to the back of the truck...and set him down gently in the cargo bay. Then he returned, picked up Nick, and did the same thing. When he had placed Connor in the back of the truck, too, the mud-creature turned and shuffled back into the cavern.

Nick jumped out the back of the truck and approached Mary Goodwin with a smile. "Golems are programmed to do one thing at a time. My guess is that guy has been loading up the deliveries for quite a few years. Kind of difficult to switch and turn him into some kind of hit man at this point. Nice try, though. Would you like to talk about the contract now?"

Mary Goodwin sighed heavily and looked at the paper again. She ran a crooked little finger along the paper as she read aloud. "Hazard pay...compound interest... health insurance...quarterly payments...retirement benefits...and—wait, you want me to split the profits for each delivery with him fifty-fifty? Are you serious?"

Nick had seen the suitcase stuffed full of cash that Connor had brought back from the delivery. Even split-ting that in half, he and his family would be rich.

And he should have enough left over to pay Nick and Burger a nice wage, of course.

"You may not have noticed—living out here in the woods like this—but the world has changed in the last few centuries. Increased law enforcement, radar-detection technologies, rapid communications across the globe." Nick cleared his throat. "Mr. Flanagan assumes a great deal more risk than his predecessors whenever he makes a delivery. This is a highly skilled position. If you want him to keep doing it, he deserves adequate compensation."

Mary Goodwin tsk-tsked and turned her attention back to the paper. "Now, what's this—you want him to be able to use the delivery truck for personal reasons? Once every six months?"

Nick grinned and nodded. Connor had promised that he would take Nick and his mom to Hawaii—the special map showed lots of wormholes on the islands. It would be her first vacation that he could ever remember. They would sit on the beach and celebrate the fact that she could quit one of her jobs. Nick couldn't wait to see the look on her face.

Mary Goodwin sighed. "You really expect me to sign on for all of this?"

Nick shrugged. "It's not the sixteen hundreds any-more, ma'am. Unions have been invented. Workers have rights."

Mary Goodwin scoffed. "I don't care what year it is. This just isn't the way secret magical agreements are made, boy."

"It is if you want Connor and us to do any more work for you."

"And *us?*"

"That's correct." Nick reached over and tapped the bottom of the paper. "As it clearly states here, anytime Connor needs help with a delivery, with any kind of magical cargo, he will have your permission to get in touch with and allow us to assist him." Nick smiled again. "For a healthy percentage of the proceeds, of course."

Mary Goodwin looked past Nick at Connor. "I've always treated your family right, Flanagan. Always. And this is how you repay me?"

"Mrs. Goodwin, my father passed away after a lifetime of working for you, and he had nothing to show for it." Connor stood up a little straighter. "I will carry on his work, but I will not dishonor his memory by letting you continue to take advantage of our family."

"Oh, I almost forgot!" Burger pulled a wrinkled piece of paper out of his pocket. "I have some demands of my own."

"*You're* making demands, too?" Mary Goodwin sneered.

Burger shrugged. "I guess it's more like just some stuff I want you to make for me."

The woman rolled her eyes and looked at the paper. "Antigravity shoes?"

Burger smiled and nodded. "So I can slam-dunk a basketball. And make sure they don't stop working at midnight or whatever. That's lame."

Mary Goodwin grumbled and looked at the paper

again, her flesh continuing to drip down her face like cold syrup. "Never-ending bag of potato chips . . . combination bike ejector seat with backpack parachute . . . there must be twenty things on this list."

"Yeah. I don't really care about the money, but it would be so awesome to have that stuff."

Mary Goodwin handed the paper back to Burger and used both hands to push the sagging, dimpled flesh up on her cheeks . . . but when she let go it all drooped down her cheeks again. And then no matter how much she gathered up the skin and pressed it in place, muttering incantations, it hung back down again. Finally she gave up and just stood there, defeated, looking every year of her four centuries.

Mary Goodwin harrumphed. Then she fixed Nick with her baleful stare. "I get the feeling that you and I ain't seen the last of each other, boy."

Nick smiled. "For the right price, ma'am, you can see me all you like."

The hag sneered. "Then I guess you boys win. This time." Then, with quicker reflexes than he ever would have thought possible for such an ancient lady, she grabbed his wrist, whipped out a long hunting knife, and opened up a gash on his index finger.

Using Nick's finger like a ballpoint pen, Mary Goodwin signed the contract with his blood and then thrust the paper back at him. Nick stared at it, his stomach doing a quick little dance of nerves. He had gotten what he wanted, but he couldn't help thinking that he would end up paying a price as well. But that was business.

"There'll be another delivery in two weeks," Mary Goodwin said. "Brand-new cargo. We load up on midnight of the next full moon. Don't be late." And with that, she turned and shuffled back into her shack and slammed the door.

Nick returned to the truck and held up the paper. "Well, gentlemen, it looks like we have the job."

Connor opened up the passenger-side door and motioned for the boys to climb in. "Let's get you two home. You must be exhausted."

Burger jumped into the truck and grabbed the special map, tracing his finger over the little flashes of neon light. "You think any of these wormholes opens up next to a pizza place? Magical adventures make me starving."

Nick and Connor laughed. "We'll see what we can do," said Connor. The delivery truck's engine fired up, and it plowed through the holly bushes and into the night.